PUCK DROP

UTAH FURY HOCKEY BOOK ONE

BRITTNEY MULLINER

CONTENTS

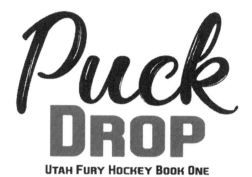

UTAH FURY HOCKEY BOOK ONE

ALSO BY BRITTNEY MULLINER

Romance

Utah Fury Hockey

Puck Drop (Reese and Chloe)

Match Penalty (Erik and Madeline)

Line Change (Noah and Colby)

Attacking Zone (Wyatt and Kendall)

Buzzer Beater (Colin and Lucy)

Open Net (Olli and Emma)

Full Strength (Grant and Addison)

Royals of Lochland

His Royal Request

Young Adult

Begin Again Series

Begin Again

Live Again

Love Again (Coming Soon)

Charmed Series

Finding My Charming

Finding My Truth (Coming Soon)

Standalones

The Invisibles

PUCK DROP:

Rule 613 (a)
Play shall start when one of the officials drops the
puck between the sticks of two opposing players

(per USA Hockey Rulebook,
https://www.usahockeyrulebook.com/)

1

CHLOE

There was nothing like watching the guys practice together for the first time at the beginning of the season. They were a family, and we'd been apart all summer. Everything was back to being how it should be, though.

The arena was almost ready for the new season. The Fury logo had been repainted and the sponsors had been updated. The fresh, gleaming ice reflected the fresh start. We had a lot to live up to. Two championships put a target on our backs, but we could handle it.

I was huddled in my red and black Fury hoodie watching George, the team photographer, on the ice. He promised me he'd get all of the shots I needed for the blog, but I was dying to get out there with him and check.

Too bad it would cause a complaint fest with the Pride, the group of players' wives and girlfriends. They tended to make every little thing the ignition to a drama fire. Most of them understood my position with the team, but a few liked to throw tantrums over me having more access than them.

The players didn't need that today of all days. There was enough on their minds.

Maybe I wouldn't have to get all the way on the ice. I'd just talk to him from the side.

Before anyone could ask me where I was going, I stood and hurried down the stairs to the glass.

George had his back to me, so I pounded until I got his attention. He dropped his camera from his face just in time to roll his eyes but walked over to me.

"What?" He had to shout to be heard over the sound of sticks slapping the ice.

"Are you getting individual action shots?"

"Yes, Chloe." He said with disdain but couldn't hide a smirk.

"Even the new guys?" I'd need pictures of them for their introduction on the team blog.

"Yes. Now let me do my job." He waved me off and pulled his camera back to his face.

"Thank you." I shouted it and knew he heard me despite his lack of reaction.

None of the women said anything to me when I took my seat, so I opened my laptop and got back to work. Writing about hockey and our team professionally was a dream come true. These guys were my life, and I'd spend all my time here anyway, so getting paid for it was amazing. Plus, it was one step closer to my ultimate goal of managing the team's charity foundation.

I'd just started a new page about the captain when someone tapped my shoulder. I forced a smile before turning around.

"Erik looks great. Did he spend the whole offseason in the gym?" Sasha, Porter Vaugh's wife, asked while eyeing him. She was beautiful with long red hair. A total vixen.

When I first met her, I pegged her as a trophy wife. A former Miss America who met Porter at a charity event. She proved me wrong though. She was smarter than she let on. She was the brain behind Porter's brand. With her help, he'd become one of the most famous players in the league.

Normally, I didn't appreciate people talking about my brother like he was a piece of meat, but I'd learned over the years that she was harmless. She checked out the guys as players. Sizing them up and searching for weaknesses that needed improvement.

"You know him. I tried to convince him to go to Mexico with me, but he refused to take time off."

"That's why he's the best." Emma, Olli Letang's wife, leaned forward and smiled. She was the polar opposite of Sasha. Petite with honey blonde hair and as sweet and reserved as they come. She hated the limelight but supported Olli whenever the occasion called for it. I knew she would prefer to be at home with a book, but she came to every practice for her husband.

She was right. Erik wasn't the best left wing in the league from luck. He'd been dedicated to the sport since the first time he laced up his skates.

"All of the guys look great. Hopefully we can find our groove with the new guys and win another championship."

Emma and Sasha beamed. There was nothing better than winning for our guys, and they earned it from the blood, sweat, and tears they put into last season. Plus, it was easier to live with them when they were winning.

I turned around and ignored the chatter of the other girlfriends and wives and focused on the guys. They were running drills, finding their feet, and getting comfortable with each other again. We had gotten a few draft picks and some trades this season that were going to need a few practices to find their flow, but overall, the team was looking great.

"Chloe, we got a code bimbo." Emma nudged me. I looked up to her and she pointed at the portal to our left. A bleach blonde wearing barely-there shorts was making her way down the stairs in precariously high heels.

I narrowed my eyes and watched her pause and wave with both arms to someone on the ice. I followed her gaze to one of the rookies. He wasn't waving back, but he'd stopped skating and was looking back at her—with panic in his eyes.

"Duty calls, ladies." I shut my laptop and slid it into my bag before standing and making my way down the row.

"Go get her."

"You show her, Chloe."

"Rookie mistake."

I ignored the comments of the Pride and focused on my target. The rookie, I think his name was Adam, knew better than to bring a groupie to practice. The guys made the rules clear for the newbies. No wonder he looked like he'd been caught.

When I was close, the bimbo looked at me and her smile disappeared. My resting face had that effect on people. Erik told me I didn't come across as an overly nice or welcoming person when people first meet me, but I couldn't help it.

When I was a few feet from her, I stopped. "How can I help you?"

She looked from me to the ice. I watched, waiting for her attention to return.

"I'm here for Adam." She pointed as if I didn't know who she was talking about.

"These are closed practices."

"But he said—"

I held up my hand. "I'm sure he said a lot of things he didn't mean."

She narrowed her eyes. "Are you with him or something?"

"No."

"Then why do you care if I'm here."

Oh, I loved when they challenged me. "You don't belong here."

She pointed over my shoulder to the Pride. "What about them?"

"They're family."

"How do you know I'm not?" She rolled her shoulders back like she just bested me.

I looked her over and shrugged. "A feeling."

She glared at me. I smiled.

"I know everyone one of those guys. I know each of the women behind me. I also know that you don't belong here."

She opened her bubblegum pink mouth to interrupt me, but I stopped her with a look.

"We don't allow the public to be here. That's why it's a closed practice."

Her eyes darted once again to the ice. Like Adam was going to run up the stairs and back her up.

"Look, I'm sure you're great, and if Adam is interested in you, I'm happy for you guys, but we don't allow people to watch these practices. That's why it's called a closed practice. Fans are more than welcome to come to watch the open practice next week."

"I'm not a fan."

"Obviously," I muttered.

"What?"

"Frankly, I don't care who you are. You need to leave.

Please don't make me get security involved. It'll be so embarrassing for you."

With one final, scathing glare, she turned and marched up the stairs. I looked to the security guard at the next entrance and nodded in her direction. He turned and disappeared, not needing further instruction.

I sighed and crossed my arms. I didn't like having to be the bad guy all the time, but the Furies weren't back to back champions because they let distractions in. We ran a tight ship. Nothing to take the players attention off what mattered most: winning.

The Pride began clapping when I walked back, and I took a mini bow before sitting down. Throwing out the trash was sometimes uncomfortable, but I'd do just about anything for the guys.

"She looked like a fighter," Sasha said with a laugh.

I shook my head and pulled my laptop back out. "She was stubborn for sure, but we've had worse."

"Remember the one that threw herself at the glass trying to escape from security?"

I laughed. "She still has the record."

Emma and Sasha continued recounting all the past crazies while I worked on my post.

"There's the new guy." Sasha's voice raised an octave. It was enough to make me look at the ice.

Sure enough, a new player was skating around the perimeter, warming up. He passed us in a flash.

"He's fast." The women all began talking at once.

"He's cute."

"He's the new right wing."

"A late trade."

"The best."

I ignored the rest of the comments and focused on the man circling the rink.

Emma leaned forward and put her hand on my shoulder. "Reese Murray."

Two words and I was gone.

The Fury got Reese Murray?

Why didn't I know this? I was supposed to be kept up to date on all the players. It was my job for crying out loud. How had this slipped by without anyone telling me?

Murray was one of the best players in the league. He was also a notorious jerk. Not what we needed this season.

"Who did we lose for him?"

She cringed. "Horran, Merck, and Benning."

Crap. Benning was our backup goaltender. If Olli got injured we'd be pulling from the farm team. "He'd better be worth it."

Sasha rested her chin on my shoulder, a literal devil on my shoulder. "He's single."

I ignored her and focused back on my screen.

"Handsome, successful, wealthy...what more could you want?"

I shrugged, hoping she'd back off, but she was stubborn.

"Just take a look, Chloe."

I fought the urge. I really did, but the next time he came around, I may have peeked.

Fine. He was handsome.

"You know me better than that, Sasha."

"Rules are meant to be broken." She whispered, and I fought the urge to shove her away.

"One, Erik would kill him. Like, bury him in an unmarked grave."

"He'd get over it."

I shook my head. He wouldn't. "Two, I don't date players."

"Such a shame."

"And three, I work for the team. It's a conflict of interest." I wasn't sure about that one, but it seemed legitimate enough.

"No such rule, Chloe."

She couldn't know that. But maybe I was underestimating her. It wouldn't be the first time.

"The first two reasons are more than enough to keep me away from him."

She tilted her head until we were cheek to cheek. "You deserve to be happy, too, you know? Erik doesn't always have to come first."

I scowled. She was a tiny bit right, not that I'd admit It to her. I did deserve to be happy, and I was...mostly. But being with a player would bring nothing but heartbreak and drama for the team.

2
―――――

REESE

I ignored the section of women sitting in the stands. I could feel their words without hearing them. From the moment I stepped on the ice, I knew I had eyes on me—from my new team and the audience.

Everything about this place seemed off. Wrong.

The only upside to the trade was the extra zero at the end of my contract. I'd left my life, my home, my friends, and my team in Boston. With a day's notice I had to pack a suitcase and board a plane for Salt Lake City. My agent could deal with moving the rest of my stuff. It was the least he could do after not getting me out of this.

Money wasn't the only thing that mattered to me. Loyalty meant more.

I thought I was a franchise player. Boston had drafted me at eighteen and I'd been with them ever since. Seven years. We'd won a championship together.

Then we started losing.

But that wasn't my fault. The team had problems off the ice.

The Utah Fury saw our, I mean their, weakness and took

the title for the past two years. They were favorites to win again this year, and I should have been happy to be included in that. I was. I was just pissed my team had given me up.

There was a street named after me.

I'd grown into a man in that city. Given everything to them.

And they traded me.

I pushed myself harder. My legs burned, begging me to reign it in. I refused.

A whistle blew, breaking my concentration and bringing my attention to the head coach, Ryan Romney, who was standing in the center of the ice.

The rest of the team was gathering around him, so I slowed to a stop toward the back of the group.

"Welcome back, Furies. We have some new faces this season." He paused and looked at each of us as if the rest of the guys hadn't already figured it out on their own.

"We're running drills this morning." He turned to the coach next to him. "Schultz, Hartman, and Murray, you're working with Coach Rust."

With that he let the defense coach and Coach Rust take over. I waited for most of the guys to disperse before joining a huddle with my new captain.

"Romney has you three as the first line with Brassard and Jones." Hartman, the captain, didn't seem surprised by the news, but Schultz was eyeing me.

Coach Rust noticed, too. "Murray is the best in the league, Schultz. You got a problem with it deal with it on your own time. While you're here, you do what I say."

Schultz didn't give a reaction.

"I want you guys to start the drills. Run through three

player passing, and puck control. It's time to act like the leaders you are."

He dismissed us, and I met Hartman and Schultz in the center. Hartman was glaring at us. "We're going to prove Coach wrong. Aren't we?"

I nodded, and Schultz agreed.

"Good. Let's get to work." He dropped the puck and skated toward the goal without waiting for us.

I was in shape. I'd had harder practices, but the stress of being out of my element made the last two hours seem like two days. We ran through drills until my feet could do them automatically. Coach blew the whistle and told us to go stretch out.

I was on the floor with a band, stretching my hamstrings when Hartman squatted next to me.

"Come on. We have to get cleaned up for pictures."

I groaned. "On the first day?"

"They want everything updated as soon as possible, especially for the new players." Hartman had the perfect captain personality. In control, calm, and reasonable. I respected him already, and not just for his experience on the ice.

I followed them into the locker room, undressed, and showered on autopilot. I was getting dressed in my new black and red jersey when Hartman sat next to my locker.

"We're going out tonight. Team bonding and all that. I'll introduce you to the rest of the guys then."

The last thing I wanted to do was go out tonight. I wanted an ice bath and my bed. Nothing else.

My disinterest must have shown. He stood up and patted my back. "It's just dinner. It won't kill you."

No getting out of it. That was left unsaid.

I followed Hartman into the elevator and stood back

while a few others joined us. They fell into a conversation about their favorite restaurant and whether or not one pizza was better than the other.

"Murray, you've got to come with us tonight. We always kick off the season there."

I nodded. I'd figure out a way to bail later.

We got off on the third floor and I followed the black and red jerseys, feeling completely out of my element, into a conference room. The photographer had set up a plain white background and a line had formed behind him. Each time I was forced to do this it reminded me of grade school. My mom would love to purchase a set of my pictures for the wall, but thankfully they weren't for sale.

"Patric, at least attempt a smile!" A tall brunette was standing behind the shoulder of the photographer yelling at the blond defenseman.

"No." He stood there stone-faced.

"We get it, you're intimidating. We'll use that for the site, but we need some pictures of you that won't scare children."

He shot daggers at her before lifting one side of his mouth a few millimeters.

"Fine. That's what we're going to get." She patted the shoulder of the photographer and turned around. She eyed the line, smiling a few times before walking toward the back where I was.

"Erik, you look like a mess. Could you have at least combed your hair?"

Schultz gave the woman a glance and shrugged. "Nope."

She pulled a comb and a small jar out of the pocket of her hoodie and pulled on his sleeve to turn him around.

"Don't do this."

She ignored him, opening the jar and swiping at the white pomade with her finger. "Down."

To my surprise, he bent down until she could easily reach his hair. In under a minute she rubbed the product into his hair and styled it to her liking.

Who was this woman? The team stylist?

"Don't mess it up." She shot him a nasty look and continued looking down the line. She was beautiful. Her long brown hair was nearly to her thin waist. Maybe not a stylist. I'd guess cheerleader if they existed for hockey.

She passed a few of the guys with a smile before stopping. "Adam, right?"

The young, blond kid nodded enthusiastically.

"You broke a rule."

He froze, and I could feel his nerves from a few people back.

"I did?"

She nodded calmly. "You know better than to invite random women to closed practices."

The back of his neck turned red. "I..uh..." He looked around as if someone was going to jump in and help him.

She narrowed her eyes. "Don't do it again."

He nodded, and she walked past him.

She was a few feet away when her eyes met mine and her eyebrow rose. Crap. I didn't know who this crazy chick was, but I didn't want her attention on me. She marched to me and stuck out her hand. "I'm Chloe."

I looked down at her hand for a beat before extending mine. "Reese."

"You aren't going to cause any problems, are you?"

"Chloe, go easy on him. He's been here for a day."

I glanced at Hartman, who was smiling at her like she wasn't insane.

I looked back to her and forced a smile. "No, I don't intend to."

"They never do." She sized me up. "Wife?"

Huh? I coughed. "No."

"Girlfriend?"

Was she coming onto me? Who was this direct? And what right did she have asking me these questions? The expression on her face told me I didn't have a choice in answering.

"No."

"Keep it that way."

"Chloe, you can't tell him—." She held up a hand to Hartman.

"Don't cause drama, don't cause problems, win games, and we won't have a problem."

I swallowed and nodded while she kept walking, probably looking for her next victim.

"Don't mind her. Chloe is a bit intense, but she means well."

"Who is she?" Probably in public relations.

"She's the digital marketing director and the head of the Fury Pride."

That didn't make sense.

"The what?"

"The Pride is the group of wives and serious girlfriends that come to practice, help run fundraisers, and organize different activities."

I nodded. Boston had a group like that, but they didn't come to photoshoots.

"But why is she here?"

He looked at me like I was an idiot. "To monitor the photoshoot?"

"Why would a marketing director care?"

He smirked. "She's here to make sure we all stay in line."

This still wasn't making sense, and he didn't seem to realize that.

"She's a babysitter?" What had the team done to deserve that?

He barked out a laugh. "A little bit. She keeps us in check, keeps the crazies away from us, and makes sure we stay the number one team in the league."

Now he was the idiot. "Is she the one winning games?"

"Not directly, but without her we wouldn't."

"Bryan! Why are you wearing the away jersey! Get back down to the locker room and change!"

I cringed. She wasn't a babysitter, she was the team mom. A young, hot one. But still a mom.

Erik Schultz was in front of the camera and threw up an arm. "Chloe, get over here."

I turned, expecting her to bite his head off for speaking to her in such a tone, but she sighed and walked back to the front of the room.

She positioned him in front of the camera and told him to smile. When she nodded her approval at the pictures, he stepped forward and pulled her against him. He kissed the top of her head once before leaving the room.

"What?" I hadn't expected that.

Hartman turned. "What'd you say?"

I shook my head. "Is that Schultz's girl?"

He laughed. "Yeah, you could say that."

The guy in front of him, I was pretty sure his name was David, turned too. "Yeah, you better stay away from that one."

I held up my hands. "I had zero intention of doing anything but that."

David and Hartman nodded.

When Coach Romney walked in and called out her

name, I expected him to kick her out, but he pulled her in for brief hug before talking to her. Seconds later, they were laughing like old pals.

The photographer waved me forward, so I moved to the mark and waited.

He began snapping pictures while I glared. It wasn't hard to fake an intimidating expression while I thought about how I should be on the other side of the country right now.

"Smile."

I closed my eyes and took a breath. I was still a player. I was still living my dream. I opened my eyes and smiled.

He took a few more before pausing. "Chloe." He shouted and got her attention. "Take a look and let me know what you think."

She gave Coach an air kiss and made her way through the team to where a laptop was set up on a table next to the photographer. They looked down at the screen together while I looked around the room. I expected stares, but the guys were engaged in conversations amongst themselves.

I watched Chloe, trying to read her expression, but she gave no hints. She glanced up and caught me looking. Rather than looking away, I raised an eyebrow and waited.

"These look great. You have a cute smile." She grinned at me while I tried to figure out if she was being sarcastic.

"Murray, you're done. Move out." Hartman strode toward me and I stepped away on reflex.

"Sorry."

Chloe watched us with a smirk across her full lips. I couldn't figure her out—and it was driving me crazy.

3

CHLOE

I sat between Emma and Sasha at the end of the table, watching the rookies compete in an impromptu food eating contest. This wasn't even a form of hazing. Once they heard the team was footing the bill, they dug in.

"Two minutes left boys. Josh has eight slices down, Mikey has ten, and Lance has nine." Hartman was standing up shouting so all forty or so people could hear him.

The Pie, our favorite hole in the wall pizza place, was actually closed, so we had the place to ourselves. Someone in the main office usually called when the team wanted to come in, so they had notice. At first, I assumed they closed so the guys had privacy, but after one night I realized they did it for the safety of the other patrons. Some sort of contest happened each time we came. From an eating challenge to handstands to box jumps on the tables. Never a dull moment with twenty-three oversized children.

The best part about this place was that the guys could make a mess and it just added to the aesthetic. The walls were covered with signatures, drawings, and stickers. The floor was concrete, so spills weren't a big deal. A few years ago, one of the guys had broken a chair in an overly aggressive game of beer pong, and they'd nailed the chair to the wall with a picture from that night next to it. They could be destructive without worrying about leaving a mess.

Erik was sitting across from me, and Sasha was sitting next to her husband, Porter. Somehow Reese ended up at our end of the table. He'd been quiet most of the night. Not that I was surprised. He'd been a man of few words at the arena, so I hadn't expected him to change in a few hours.

We were a lot to take in, so I tried to cut him some slack. Emma and Sasha had been trying to engage him all night, but he stuck to his clipped responses.

"Time! Lance finished strong and is our winner at twelve slices!" Hartman shouted, and the group broke out in cheers.

Emma cringed. "That's more than an entire pizza."

I nearly gagged. They'd work it off tomorrow at practice, but it still didn't seem normal.

"We're getting low." Erik grabbed two pitchers from our end of the table, but I stood and took them from him.

"I'll get it."

"I'll help." Reese stood and followed me back to the counter.

"Coke, please." As much as the guys hated it, drinking wasn't an option during the season. They might be able to still get away with it this week, but they'd pay for it during workouts.

"Water for this one." Reese handed a waiter another pitcher and waited next to me.

"Thanks for grabbing that one. I would have come back for it."

I watched him shrug and wished I could get more out of him.

"You seem to take care of a lot for the team. It's the least I could do."

I leaned against the counter and faced him. "It's my job."

"It's your job to get refills, as the director of digital marketing?"

He had me there. I did it because it was habit. Taking care of Erik, and the team, was second nature to me.

"Not necessarily."

He grunted and took a pitcher the waiter had just set down in front of us. Before I could take the other two, he had them in his hands and was walking back to the table.

I followed, feeling strange coming back empty-handed. I tried to help him set them down, but he gave me one look and I backed off.

What crawled up his behind?

Emma caught my eye when I sat down and smirked. "Have a problem with chivalry?"

"I was just trying to help."

"So was he."

She had a point. Getting help wasn't something I was used to.

"Chloe, I have two suits at the cleaners. Can you pick those up tomorrow?" Erik looked at me with puppy dog eyes as if he needed to beg.

"Sure, just give me the tickets. Last time they threatened to hold your clothes hostage without it."

"They're on the counter."

I nodded and refilled my glass with soda, then picked up Erik's, Hartman's, Emma's, and reached for Reese's, but his hand shot out and brushed mine away.

"I can do it myself."

I raised a brow but kept my tone cool. "I'm sure you can, big boy. I was just trying to be nice."

His eyes narrowed. "I don't need you, or anyone, to take care of me."

I backed off and bit my lip to keep from saying anything I'd regret later.

"Just let her, Murray. It's what she loves to do." I smiled at Erik's words, but deep down I appreciated that Reese didn't expect me to do things for him like the rest of the team. I didn't mind helping them, but it was refreshing, and odd, to be told no.

I'd been taking care of Erik practically our whole lives. When we were kids, I made sure he knew when practice was and double checked his bag to make sure he remembered his skates and his favorite tape. When he moved to play in the major junior league, I sent him care packages and made sure he was staying on top of his school work.

Our parents had called me his second mom, but it was because he would forget to do things himself. As we got older, I was the one that reminded him of events he had to attend and when his assignments were due. It got worse after our parents died. Things changed from me being the second mom to the only one taking care of him. He'd always had our parents, his coaches, and then his agent doing things for him. He swore he wouldn't survive a day without me, but a small part of me regretted enabling him and allowing myself to become his crutch.

Not that I had much to complain about. His career supported me too. With his signing bonus he paid off my student debt and bought our penthouse apartment. He didn't just take from me. He made sure to take care of me the only way he knew how. The team had caught onto this, and I became the sister to everyone. It was a great feeling to be a part of the Fury family, but it killed my dating life.

I'd been on only a handful of dates since we moved to

Salt Lake City. Guys tend to get intimidated when they pick me up and find half a dozen professional hockey players eyeing them and threatening to cause damage if they hurt me.

It was inconvenient, but nice. What girl wouldn't love having them on their side? But it meant my life revolved around my brother and his teammates.

"She's not here to take care of me." Reese hadn't yet learned about the team dynamics, but Erik didn't look like he was going to cut him slack.

"Back off, Murray."

"I just don't get why you let your girlfriend wait on you and your teammates. It's demeaning."

I nearly broke out laughing at how mixed up he was, until I heard the last word. He thought it was demeaning to refill a pitcher?

"Excuse me. Doing nice things for other people isn't demeaning. It's courteous."

He narrowed his eyes at me. "Why hasn't anyone else here been courteous? No one has to lift a finger when you're around cause they know you'll do it for them."

Erik ignored us and continued glaring at Reese. "You've got it all figured out, huh?"

A vein in Reese's neck was bulging under the skin. I looked away, hating that I noticed. "You shouldn't treat her like she's here to serve you. What kind of relationship is that?"

Erik rolled his eyes. "Dude, she's my sister."

A flash of confusion shown across his face. His eyes went to Hartman, who shrugged. "I said she was his girl. You weren't specific."

The rest of the guys around us laughed and began making unnecessary comments. Most of them knew our story. They knew how close we were because of what happened to our parents. We were the only family we had left.

"That's almost worse. You let your sister do everything for you?"

"You know what, Murray? You've been on the team for one day and all you've done is brood and judge like you're so much better than anyone else here. You're a great player, I won't deny that, but so are the rest of us. We're the back to back champions, remember? You don't know the dynamics of our team. You don't know each of our histories. Maybe stop sulking for a minute and get to know who we are and you wouldn't feel the need to look down on each of us."

I'd never seen the guys so quiet. No one moved. No one spoke. I didn't take my eyes of Reese. He leaned back in his chair and after a moment he nodded once.

He didn't say anything, but I could see in his face that at least some of what Erik said sunk in. Erik had been a bit harsh, but he'd been right to call Reese out early. The last thing the team needed was discord this early in the season, especially since they would be on the first line together. They needed to trust and respect each other in order to perform well together on the ice.

The rest of the evening was uneventful. I said goodbye to everyone, although Reese avoided me, and got into Erik's car.

We drove in silence for a few blocks before I had to break the silence.

"How do you feel about this year?" We made predictions for each season, a tradition we started his very first year. I always tried to be optimistic, saying we'd win the championship, but Erik had a much more realistic perspective and was usually more accurate. Although, the last two years he said he felt like the team was going to make it.

With the trades and new recruits, I was interested in how he felt.

"As long as we can find our groove we should be fine."

That wasn't the response I'd been expecting. Fine wasn't a championship. Fine wasn't what Erik ever wanted.

"There will be some growing pains with the new guys, but you looked great at practice." Erik shrugged and pulled into the parking garage of our building.

I followed him to the elevator and remained silent on the way up to our home. Maybe it was a twin thing, or maybe it was the result of spending your whole life with someone, but I'd learned when to push Erik to talk and when to accept that he needed to be in his head.

He was a leader. He would find a way to fix things with Reese and work with him. He had to.

I watched him disappear down the hall and into his room. He'd figure things out and hopefully be back to himself tomorrow. I went to the kitchen and made some tea before grabbing my laptop and heading to my room. I wanted to go through the practice pictures from today and send George the photos I wanted to use so he would have them edited tomorrow.

I scrolled through, starring the ones I liked until I found one of Reese. The determination in his eyes was almost scary. He had the puck and was about to hit it. He wasn't looking down at it though, he was looking straight ahead. His control and confidence were evident.

This was how I wanted to introduce him to our fans. I wanted them to get behind him and make him feel welcome to a new city. Erik had never been traded, but I'd seen enough guys come through that I knew feeling accepted was important. Very few of the guys would ever admit to it aloud, but I could see their countenance change the second the crowd chanted their name. They needed to know that their new city believed in them, and it was my job to market them to the fans and get them to adore the players before they ever see them. By opening night of the season, I would have the crowds chanting Reese's name.

4

REESE

I was tense walking into the locker room the next day, but Hartman immediately slapped my back and a few of the guys greeted me. I put on my pads and skates and followed the guys out to the ice. I could tell Erik was still mad about what I said at dinner, but to his credit, he didn't take it out on me. He didn't ignore my calls for passes. He didn't even slam me into a wall when he had the chance. I gained a bit of respect for him. Any player that can leave the problems at the door deserves that.

Coach Rust worked us hard, and when the final whistle blew, I was ready to collapse. I was amazed the guys could take these practices without being too sore to play come game day. I'd have to up my game or invest in an ice maker to keep my bathtub filled.

"Murray." Ah there it was.

I stopped in the tunnel and waited for Erik to catch up to me. I turned to face him when he was at my side.

"You upset Chloe last night."

I fought to keep the smirk off my lips. He was talking like

a mobster. I was waiting for him to say I had a meeting with his cousin Vinny off Pier Thirteen.

He glared at me. "I don't appreciate the way you spoke to her."

As if I was the one with the problem.

I took a step closer. He didn't intimidate me the way he thought he did. "I don't appreciate how you take advantage of her."

His eyes narrowed to slits. "You don't know anything about us."

I clenched my fist but forced myself to relax. Punching a teammate wouldn't be a great way to start my time on the team.

"I know that you expect her to do everything for you. You don't lift a hand when she's around. A good relationship is about respect, and I can tell you don't respect her."

Erik got in my face. Like he was about to lose it too. "You don't know what you're talking about."

Hartman stepped between us then, forcing us apart. "Guys. You both need to relax."

"He crossed a line." Erik jabbed a finger at my chest.

Hartman held his hands up before I could protest. "Look. You're both in the wrong." He looked to me. "You can't come into a new group, a new team, and make assumptions." He turned to Erik. "You need to relax, and maybe you could try to do something for Chloe every so often."

Erik was about to speak, but Hartman stopped him.

"Now kiss and make up."

I rolled my eyes, but he looked at each of us waiting expectantly.

Erik didn't seem like he was the type to make the first move, and I didn't want to stand here any longer than necessarily. The showers were screaming my name.

I swallowed and took a slow breath. There was no point in creating a rivalry. We needed to work together. It was his business. If Chloe put up with it, that was on her.

"Erik, I'm sorry that I made assumptions about how you treat Chloe. You guys are right. I'm new here and I don't know your relationship. I'll apologize to Chloe as well."

Hartman nodded his approval, and Erik seemed to think for a moment before nodding. "I'm sorry for getting angry at you. You're right." He glanced at Hartman before continuing. "I should be more appreciative of Chloe. She does a lot for me. She always has. I guess I've just gotten too used to it."

"I'm glad things are cleared up. Now hit the showers. You guys stink."

I didn't need to be told that again. Within twenty minutes, I was clean and on my way up to the front office.

I smiled at the woman at the front desk and walked past her with confidence, so she wouldn't stop me. I had no idea where I was going, but I figured the chances were low an office employee would stop a player from wandering around.

"Hey." I ignored the call behind me, hoping they weren't talking to me. "Murray."

I turned to see Mr. Snow, the general manager, walking toward me.

"Hello, sir. How are you?" I'd only met him briefly at the press conference announcing my trade. I'd been jet lagged and still fuming about leaving my home, so I wasn't sure I'd made the best impression. Mr. Snow didn't seem to mind though.

"I'm great! How are you settling in? Are the coaches taking good care of you? Is there anything that you need?"

"No, sir. I've been well taken care of."

His enthusiasm was a tad over the top. If I were a diva like some of my old teammates, I'd take advantage of his generosity and make ridiculous demands, but that wasn't my style. I preferred to be low maintenance. I found that it helped me get what I really wanted, when it counted.

Well, up until I got traded.

"I'm glad to hear it, Murray. If there's ever anything."

"Thank you, sir."

I sidestepped him and looked around for Chloe. I almost walked past her office, but her voice caught my attention.

"No, the report was due by noon. You know this. It's a weekly thing, Craig."

I glanced into the office, and since she was on the phone, she didn't notice me until I knocked on the open door. She glanced up and looked confused. She waved me in and hung up her call.

"Hi, Reese."

"Hey."

She smiled at me, looking uncertain. "What can I do for you?"

I looked around her office, which was decorated in hockey memorabilia. There were a few signed posters. One of Gretzky, Orr, and even Crosby. The majority though was only one player—Erik Schultz.

She had pictures of him from PEEWEE, high school, and college.

"I talked to Erik after practice."

She cringed.

"He made some valid points. We uh...we worked things out, but I felt like I owed you an apology too."

Her eyes shot up in surprise. "You really don't have to—"

"No, I do. I made assumptions about your relationship. I jumped to conclusions rather than getting to know either of you. I'm obviously way behind and I'm trying to get to know the dynamics on the team. I just should have learned more about the situation before butting in."

She smiled and folded her hands on her desk. "Honestly, it was sweet. I've taken care of Erik our whole lives. I think sometimes he forgets I'm his sister, not his mom."

"Sorry for the whole girlfriend thing, too."

She laughed. "Did someone tell you something else?"

I rubbed my jaw. "Not directly. I guess, I assumed it."

"You're pretty bad at making assumptions."

I nodded slowly. It had never been a problem in the past, but even since getting here it was one thing after another. Maybe it was just Chloe. She was affecting me.

"I'm sorry."

She shook her head and smiled. "No need. It's not like Erik or I clarified that for you. I just thought that Hartman would have given you the rundown on the team."

"He kind of did. Well, with the guys."

"Sometimes I forget that I'm not one of them." She winked. "I'm usually treated like one."

"I don't think I could ever do that." I hadn't meant to be so honest, but something about her big brown eyes pulled words from my mouth.

Watching her cheeks turn red was worth it though. I'd embarrass myself every day for the rest of my life to see that.

She cleared her throat and looked away. "How are you liking things here?"

I shrugged. "It's been fine."

"Not home, though?"

I shook my head. "Not yet."

"Well, I've been here for a while. If you ever want me to show you around..."

Her voice trailed off as my brain went into overdrive. She

was being polite. She worked for the team. She was just doing her job.

"Oh." It would be a terrible idea. She was Erik's sister, and he wasn't my number one fan. Going out with her would only make things between us worse. That was the last thing the team needed. It was the last thing I needed to do when I was trying to find my place. Hockey always came first. No matter how gorgeous the offer was. "I don't think so."

"Oh." The shock in her voice threw me off. She expected me to accept the offer? Didn't she see how bad that would make things for me? For the team?

"I just don't want to—"

She held up her hands. "You don't have to explain. I get it."

I doubted she did.

"I should get going." I stood up, and she didn't stop me. "I'm sorry again, about yesterday."

She was biting her lip when I turned back to the doorway. On the way to the elevator I sighed and dodged any other office employees.

I hated leaving her there thinking the worst. She didn't get that she was automatically off limits. Maybe if Erik and I got along, I could get his permission, but right now I needed to prove myself to him as a teammate. Getting personal would come later.

5

CHLOE

What just happened?

That was humiliating.

We'd had a moment. We were laughing. Smiling. How had I read it so wrong? It's not like I asked him out. I was offering to show him around the city. I'd offered to do it for every guy who joined the team. Granted, Erik was usually with me. I'd never been shut down though.

I turned to my computer and opened the page on the blog where I'd written his welcome post. Our fans loved the honest, yet comical voice I wrote these with. I wanted each player to become real to them. I wanted them to feel like they knew them as a person rather than just jerseys.

This time, I was going to be brutally honest.

Reese Murray comes to the Utah Fury from the Boston Sailors after six years with the team. He was a top draft pick of 2012 and joined the NHL at just eighteen years old. He's won one championship and hopes to win another with the Fury.

I stared at the screen. This was the basic information I provided for all trades. Now was the time to get personal.

While we're excited to have his talent join our team this

season, we're left wanting. All the talent in the world won't make up for his personality. He's somber. He's evasive. Maybe he left his personality in Boston. He's gruff, abrasive, and judgmental. He's not getting along with the team because he isn't trying. Maybe he's still sore about the trade, or maybe he's just a brooding jerk.

The jury is still out.

I hit publish before I could change my mind.

The fans deserved to know the truth. I could sugarcoat it all day long, but what was the point? People would see the truth as soon as they saw him at events, signings, and on the ice. He wasn't trying. It was like he was going through the motions on autopilot. It was a privilege to be on this team. He needed to pull his head out of wherever he shoved it and realize that.

I was willing to give people second chances. Especially under his circumstances. He'd been traded without warning. I couldn't image what Erik, or I, would do in that situation. Erik would be pissed. Something would end up broken.

I could forgive the scene at The Pie. I could move past it and accept his apology, but why did he turn around and reject me? I was trying to be helpful. Extend the olive branch. Shutting me down before I could even explain was borderline insulting.

He deserved what I wrote.

As soon as he proved he was different from my first and second impression of him, I'd change it.

"Chloe." My boss, Mr. Truman, bellowed my name from his office.

How had he already read it? I smoothed my skirt when I stood and walked to the office next to mine. "Yes, Mr. Truman?" I smiled as innocently as I could.

"Take it down."

"What?" Always, always plead ignorance.

He narrowed his eyes. "Take down his bio."

"It was completely accurate." I stood my ground, refusing to let him intimidate me.

"Maybe to you, after a bad experience, but you wrote him in a horrible light. You're supposed to support him. He's on our team, Chloe." The vein in the center of his forehead was pulsing. I'd only seen that happen once before. The person that caused it no longer worked here.

"I'm leaving it up until he proves me wrong."

"Chloe." He used his exasperated voice. I'd heard it a hundred times before. It was a tool he tried to use on me. I knew better.

"Dale."

He dropped his head into his hands, massaging his temples. "This is not going to make management happy."

As if he cared. The general manager and owners loved me. I'm sure in the small chance that they read the bio I wrote that they wouldn't care.

"Dale, it will be fine. I'll write a retraction once he proves he deserves it. I've always been honest, and the fans know that."

He continued rubbing. "I'm not going to change your mind."

"Nope." I popped my lips.

"You're going to drive me to an early grave." I turned and walked away before he could change his mind. "Survived four kids and this is what kills me."

I laughed to myself and returned to my desk. I had more important things to work on than player bios. Mine weren't even the official ones for the team site. They were just on the blog.

People would move on. I had to focus on the first team event.

Sales had been great for the past four seasons, especially with two championships, but awareness could always be improved. The city needed to know that the team was dedicated to improving what they could and being advocates. The first event was a charity dinner. It was black tie and cost one thousand dollars a plate. It was more of a glorified photo opportunity and a way for the rich in the area to rub elbows with their favorite athletes.

The guys hated it, but they were good sports about it. The one night brought in over three hundred grand with the cost per guest plus donations. It was a big deal for the team, and the Fury foundation, and this year's event was in three days.

I needed to call each vendor and confirm they would be on time. Plus, I needed to get each player to confirm they would be there. There were always a few that put up a fight, and I needed to get them on board so they had time to get a tux.

A few hours later and I'd made my way through the list and took a breath. Everything was going according to plan. It took a few years, but I'd finally developed a plan to make these events run smoothly.

"Have a good night, Chloe." I looked up to see Kristen, my assistant, standing in my doorway.

"Is it that time already?" I checked my clock and groaned. It was already seven. I needed to get down to the locker room before everyone left.

She laughed. "Yes, Chloe. It's time to stop for the day."

I nodded and shut my laptop. I tended to work long hours simply because I lost track of time. If it weren't for

Kristen and Erik reminding me to eat, sleep, and take breaks I'd never leave my office.

"Okay, have a good night."

Kristen nodded and walked toward the elevator. Erik hadn't texted me yet, so they must still be in practice. I gathered my things and headed down to the ice. This way no one could get away without me reminding them about the event.

6

REESE

We were taking a quick break between flow exercises the following day and I took the time to down an entire bottle of water. A few of the guys were surrounding Dumphy, a defensive man, and he was reading something from his phone. They broke out in laughter and all turned to me at the same time. I turned to look around, but I was standing by myself. Hartman slid down the bench until he was next to me.

"What'd you do?"

I shook my head. "No idea."

He looked back at the group. "No recent arrests?"

"Nope." I tossed my empty bottle in my bag.

"Any embarrassing hookups lately?"

Ha. As if I had the time. "No."

Hartman stood and skated over to the group. Dumphy handed over his phone and after a moment Hartman's laughter reached me. Great.

He handed the phone back and came back over. "You're not going to like this, dude."

Probably not, at least if the laughter was any indication.

"What'd you do to piss off Chloe?"

I shrugged. "Nothing."

He nodded slowly. "Apparently, you did, and she wrote about it on the team blog."

"There's a team blog?"

He nodded again. "Yeah, the fans love it. Chloe writes funny stories and behind the scenes stuff that doesn't make it onto the social media accounts."

"And she wrote something bad about me?"

He shrugged. "It's not necessarily bad. She just wrote about her first impression of you."

Which wasn't great.

"So, all the fans already hate me?"

He laughed and patted my shoulder. "I doubt your jersey will sell out on opening night."

A whistle sounded, and I'd never been happier to start practice. Running drills would be the perfect thing to keep my mind occupied.

I felt the eyes of the rest of the team on me for the next hour. Any time Erik was near me, he shoved me. So, I was wrong about him leaving problems at the door.

It was grueling, and all I wanted to do was get away.

Practice was finally called, and I didn't waste a second getting off the ice and into the locker room first. I wanted to shower and get home without having to talk to anyone else.

My plan didn't make it. The hoots and mocking started as soon as my shower did. I ignored it.

Hartman was sitting in front of my locker when I went back to undress. "Come on. What'd you do?"

I ignored him and grabbed my clothes. I took one step before he grabbed my elbow. "I don't like contention on the team this early in the season. We haven't even had a game yet and there's issues. So, tell me, what did you do?"

37

He wasn't asking me as a friend like he had before. This was my captain asking.

"She offered to show me around town and I told her no thanks."

His eyes narrowed. "Were you polite?"

"I think so."

He stood so we were eye to eye. "She wouldn't have gotten upset about that, Murray. You had to have done something else."

I shrugged. "That's the only thing I can think of."

"Chloe is like a sister to me, to most of us. If you have a problem with her or you hurt her you'll end up having issues with all of us."

I understood his threat and gave a quick nod. He dropped his hand. "You need to fix this."

"How? Are you telling me to go out with her? I thought that would be the thing to cause issues, that's why I turned her down."

"You're pretty quick to assume that she was asking you out." He was talking down to me like a child.

"Why else would she be asking me?"

He smirked. "You're a cocky little idiot, aren't you?"

I wanted to be insulted, but it was more of a joke to himself.

"She offers every guy that joins the team the same thing. Usually she takes them all out together. If you pulled your head out of your skate, you would have heard the rookies and the other trades talking about it at practice today."

And just like that I was the team joke. "I didn't know."

"Obviously." He shook his head. "Chloe is an amazing person and there is nothing more important to her than the success of her brother and the team."

I nodded. I wasn't used to having anyone like that. Most

people that hung around my last team were angling for personal gain. A person like Chloe was unheard of.

"I'll apologize."

"Good. Now hurry and get dressed. She's waiting to talk to all of us."

"She's here?"

"Yup, we need to get to the meeting room."

I got dressed in record time and joined the rest of the guys just before Chloe walked in. She smiled at everyone, but it slipped the moment her eyes met mine. It lasted a fraction of a second, but it was long enough to make me feel like a complete jerk.

"As most of you know, we host a fundraiser the weekend before the first game." She paused as a few of the guys groaned. She shot them a look but smiled and continued. "This Saturday night is the gala. It's black tie, so please make sure your tux is dry cleaned and tailored." She scanned the team, stopping and giving pointed looks at a few of the guys. They must be routine offenders.

"This is a big night for the community, the team, and the Fury Foundation. We raised three hundred and five thousand last year, so let's try to beat that. Which means you all need be on your best behavior. Smile, talk, be gracious hosts."

She scanned the group with a small smile. "Any questions?"

There were a few grumbles, but no one said anything. I raised my hand then felt stupid, so I spoke up. "Can you tell us new guys what the foundation does?"

She smiled, and it lit up her whole face. "Yes, of course. The Fury Foundation helps with the community. When it was founded, the board couldn't agree on one cause to focus on, so they decided to spread out the funds throughout the community by improving parks, funding shelters, providing supplies and food. Charities in the area reach out with their needs and we do our best to fulfill them."

I was surprised by how passionate she was when talking about it. She loved this foundation. Coach stepped forward and excused us while hanging back to talk to Chloe. I remained in my chair and waited for everyone to file out of the room. Soon, it was just me and Chloe.

I stood and walked to the front of the room and waited as she gathered her things. When she turned and saw me waiting she hesitated, but finally pasted on a smile. "Hi, Reese, what can I do for you?"

"I wanted to apologize about before. I..." I blew out a breath and rubbed my hand through my hair. "I didn't know it was something you do for all the new guys."

She raised an eyebrow. "You thought I was asking you out?"

Why did she have to make it seem like such a ridiculous possibility? "Yeah, I did."

She tilted her face up toward me and smirked. "I'm sorry I gave you the wrong impression, Reese. I should have clarified that it was a group thing. I don't date players."

I fought to not react to her words. She just shot me down.

"Of course. Well, I'm sorry again about what I said, and for anything else I've done wrong already."

She couldn't have known that I already knew about the bio she wrote, but I hoped she knew I was being sincere.

"I appreciate it, Reese. I have to go." She left the room, and I watched her walk to the elevator.

She let me off too easily. Either she didn't believe me or she didn't care, but if she didn't care she wouldn't have taken it out on my bio. I had to do something to get her to see I wasn't the gruff guy she thought I was. Second chances were hard to get, but I was going to make it happen.

I hurried down the hall and into the parking garage. Erik's car was gone, but Olli and Hartman were standing in front of their cars talking. I walked over as their conversation ended.

Olli noticed me first. "Hey, Murray."

"Hi, guys. I...umm...I need to fix something."

Hartman nodded. He wasn't gloating but that didn't mean it wouldn't come later. "What do you need?"

"Can you tell me something I can get Chloe to apologize?"

Olli laughed. "You can't buy her forgiveness. She's not that type."

"Unlike, Sasha." Hartman laughed.

Olli nodded. "Porter is a lucky man. One call to his jeweler and he's out of the dog house."

Great. They were both zero help.

I turned to leave, but Hartman stopped me. "She's been talking nonstop about some show that's coming to town. I guess it's impossible to get tickets to. If you can manage that, I think she'd forgive you for just about anything."

That sounded like something I could handle. "What show?"

He shrugged. "The really popular one? People are always talking about it."

He looked to Olli who nodded. "The one about the founding fathers. Emma and I saw it in New York last year and Chloe's been dying to see it."

"Thanks, guys."

I turned and walked to my car. If I was back home I knew exactly who I could call to get tickets. I had friends there, connections. I didn't have the slightest idea where to start here.

Once I was in my car I scrolled through my phone for my assistant, Bryce. I rarely asked him for things like this. I didn't have him move out here. He could manage things from Boston, and I didn't want to make him uproot his life.

"Hey, Reese."

"Bryce, I need a favor."

"That's a first."

No kidding. "I need tickets to a show here."

He laughed. "And what do you expect me to do?"

"Figure it out." I snapped and instantly regretted it. He didn't deserve me taking out my frustration on him.

"Dude, calm down. Text me the show and dates that work and I'll see what I can do."

I took a breath. "Thanks. I owe you."

"Yes, more than you could ever repay me."

I hung up and sent him the information. Hopefully he would come through for me. I needed to get on Chloe's good side for the sake of the team.

7

CHLOE

I'd tripled checked everything. My team of assistants and interns were on top of it. Tonight would be fine. No. It would be perfect. I told myself these things over and over on my drive back to my house to get ready for the gala.

"Are you serious?" I was running around, making calls, and generally freaking out all day while Erik was sitting on the couch wearing sweatpants watching TV.

He tore his eyes off the screen long enough to glance at me. "What?"

"You need to get ready. I told you we need to leave at five." I checked the clock. Less than an hour to get ready and he was sitting on the couch.

"It will take me less than fifteen minutes. Chill out."

He wasn't wrong, but his calmness was irritating.

"Sorry that I've been working my butt off all day, no, all month, organizing this event and I'm a little stressed out."

He turned off the TV and flung the remote on the couch. "You did this to yourself. You asked to be the head of the charity board."

It was true, but that wasn't what I wanted to hear. "Just

go get ready, please."

He wandered into his room at a pace that irritated me, but I kept my mouth shut. He was doing it on purpose and I wasn't going to be baited today. Sometimes, living with my brother wasn't worth the headaches he caused.

My dress was hanging in my closet waiting for me. I checked the clock while pulling half of my hair into a bun on top of my head. No time to wash and dry. Second-day hair would have to do.

"Are you done yet?" I peeked out of my bathroom as Erik let himself into my room and flung himself on my bed, landing on his back.

"Don't lay down! Your tux will wrinkle." I would have gone over and pulled him off, but my hair was attached to a curling iron.

"I'll be fine. Are you almost done?"

My hair was half curled and I was standing in my robe, but at least my makeup was finished. "Give me ten minutes."

He rolled to his side to face me. "You have five."

I wrapped a new section of hair and waited for it to get hot to the touch. If I hadn't thrown myself into this mess, I could have been getting pampered by a team. Oh no. I had to go and ask to be in charge of the events.

It was the position I really wanted, rather than social media, but the front office didn't think it was a fulltime position. I was determined to get them to see it was, but I was digging my grave by having everything go smoothly. I'd convince them things would be better and we'd get more donations if I could dedicate my attention to this alone.

"Three minutes."

"Stop it!" I ran my fingers through the curls to soften them then sprayed an obscene amount of hairspray to keep everything in place.

I pulled the dress off its hanger and shut the bathroom door to change. I'd gone with a black evening gown with a high neckline to please Erik. I'd shown him when I got home from the store a few weeks ago and he approved. What he hadn't seen was the thigh-high slit in the front and the plunging keyhole below the neckline.

It was sexy without screaming any body parts in your face.

I slipped on my heels, touched up my lipstick, and stepped into my room. Erik looked up from his phone and groaned.

"You didn't show me that dress."

"Yes, I did."

He narrowed his eyes. "Next time, I'm making you take it out of the bag."

I smirked and waltzed past him. "Let's go."

We made it on time, just a few cars back in line. I'd wanted to rent a limo, or at least have a driver for the evening, but Erik refused to let anyone else drive his Lamborghini Centenario. Not even me. Not that I'd ever want to be responsible for it. I could work every day for the rest of my life at my current job and not have enough to buy it. No thanks.

It was also the one thing in the world, besides me and hockey, that he loved.

The valet motioned us forward, but when he held up his hand for us to stop, Erik laughed and drove past him to park the car himself next to the Mercedes, Ferraris, and Rolls Royces of the other players. Apparently, none of the guys wanted someone else touching their babies.

Erik got out first and immediately the snap of dozens of cameras greeted him. He walked around the car and opened my door, and the paparazzi followed. I stepped away so he could pose for a few seconds next to his car before taking his elbow and moving him to the red carpet.

Rich people loved walking on red carpets. If it were up to the team they'd meet at the Pie and each write a check with a few zeros at the end to avoid nights like these, but management loved the publicity the team got.

Erik and I posed our way down the line until I heard calls for solo shots of him. Finally, I could get into the event. I was going crazy not knowing how things were going.

"Sorry." He broke away and hit his normal poses while the camera flashes when crazy.

I smiled as I entered the ballroom. Everything looked great. I spotted my assistant, Kristen, and made my way to her.

"Any fires?"

She shook her head. "Everything is fine, like I told you it would be."

I scanned the room. The food was stocked. Waiters were walking around with drinks and hor d'oeuvres.

"Did you remind security to check the lists? I don't want anyone getting in that shouldn't."

She gave me a condescending look. "Yes, Chloe."

"I'm serious. I can't handle throwing people out tonight."

"Chloe, we have this under control. Go enjoy yourself and schmooze the guests. We need donations." She winked and turned, leaving me alone.

She was right. I was here for one purpose tonight. Get donations for the Fury Foundation. I straightened my shoulders and plastered on my hostess smile and roamed the room, smiling and greeting the guests.

My studying had paid off and I was able to greet everyone by name, and even remembered a few children and grandchildren's names just to suck up a bit more. People loved being remembered, and it was my job to make each of them feel like the most important person in the room. Sure, most of them were here to rub elbows with the players so they could brag at their next golf or bridge game with their buddies, but I could tell it impressed them when I remembered our conversations from months or years before.

It wasn't much of a skill as it was practice.

When I got back home tonight I'd go straight to my laptop to write down discussion points in each person's folder. Oh yes. There were folders.

"Mr. and Mrs. Huntsmen, so lovely to see you." I air kissed each of them and rambled on about their dogs: Fluffy, Klutzy, and Muttsy. They were an adorable elderly couple that donated generously every year and were rink side season ticket holders. They claimed watching hockey kept them young, and I couldn't argue that. They were the healthiest eighty-year-olds I'd ever met.

"Chloe, darling, I hear we have some new blood this season. How are our boys looking?" Mr. Huntsmen was looking around the room. "I have a considerable amount tied to them winning another championship."

I covered my mouth to hide my smile and leaned in. "They're looking really good. We stole Boston's secret weapon."

He leaned back with wide eyes. "Reese Murray is here? I'd heard the rumor."

He must not read the blog. Probably for the best.

I looked around and spotted Reese not too far away. I waited until he turned in my direction and gave a small wave. He looked hesitant but walked over.

"Mr. and Mrs. Huntsmen, I'd like to introduce you to the newest Fury, Reese Murray. Reese, Mr. and Mrs. Huntsmen are some of our biggest fans. They come to every home game, so you'll get used to seeing them sitting in the front of section one-eleven."

Reese turned on his charm like a switch. I watched as he won over their hearts in less than a minute.

"Is your jersey in the team store, dear?" Mrs. Huntsmen had already developed a solid crush. Erik would be so disappointed to lose his biggest fan.

"I believe it is." Reese looked to me and I nodded.

"All of the new players' jerseys are available, but I'll have one of Reese's waiting on your seat on opening night."

Mrs. Huntsmen's face lit up just like I knew it would. "Oh, Chloe, you spoil us."

I leaned in and winked. "I have to. You two are my favorites."

"Oh!" They laughed together like children before spotting another player they wanted to chat with.

Reese watched them walk away before turning to me. "You were really good with them."

I tugged at my hair once before realizing what I was doing and dropped my arms to my side. "It's my job."

He smiled, and my knees melted. He shouldn't be allowed to do that in public. If Mrs. Huntsmen had seen that she would have gone into cardiac arrest.

"I thought your job was to write inaccurate player bios."

I fought the urge to cross my arms, or even laugh. I would not get defensive, even if he did have a point. I may have written the post out of embarrassment, but I wasn't about to admit that to him.

"They are accurate based on my perception of the player."

He seemed to think that over while I scanned his body. No man should be allowed to look that good in a tux. He could be a cover model with a jaw like that. I dreaded

48

when his scruff would turn into a full beard around playoffs.

"Chloe."

My eyes snapped up to his eyes.

"I'm sorry for how I was acting my first few days. The trade completely blindsided me. I haven't handled it well." He let out a sigh. "I shouldn't have taken it out on your or anyone on the team. I'm not normally that...abrasive."

He dragged out the last word, a direct quote from my article.

I bit my bottom lip to keep from laughing and took a breath before responding. "I appreciate that. I understand too. Well, not being traded from a team, obviously. But I understand being upset when things out of your control affect your life."

He stared into my eyes for several long beats before nodding slightly. "Exactly." He broke eye contact and looked around the room. "This looks great. You did a good job."

"Thank you." I took the compliment with a smile. It was a labor of love, and after spending months planning it, the night went by in a blink. It always felt a little bittersweet.

"Do you work on all the charities for the team?"

I was a bit surprised by the questions. "I organize the events, like this, and coordinate with the foundations we support."

He nodded and motioned for a passing waiter. Reese took two flutes and handed me one. He took a sip before looking at me again. "Do you ever help any of the players with their charities?"

"Some of them. Erik and I run his together, but most of the wives take over for their husbands." His expression changed for barely a moment. I didn't answer his question. Was he wanting me to help him? He could just come out and ask. "I'm always willing to help players that need some help setting up or organizing events, though."

That seemed to brighten his mood a bit. "Interesting."

Interesting indeed. Perhaps I'll be rewriting his bio sooner than I thought.

"Chloe," Erik called out as he walked over with an empty glass in his hand.

Reese met my eyes and smiled before walking away. I'd have to find out more about why he was asking those questions later.

"Hi, Erik." I waved at a passing waiter and took a glass for my brother. He accepted it and took a large gulp before speaking.

"Everything looks great. You did a good job, sis."

"Thanks." I appreciated the validation. It was surreal when events were finally happening after planning them for so long. I often had to remind myself to stop and enjoy the moment.

"So, I have a dilemma."

I narrowed my eyes and waited. This usually didn't lead to a good thing.

"I know that I'm your ride and all, but I..."

I held up my hand knowing exactly where this was going. "I'll find a ride or call a cab."

He stepped forward and gave me a brief hug. "You're the best."

I fought the urge to roll my eyes. "Do me a favor and go to her place."

There had been one too many awkward morning moments of me running into the girl during her attempt at a quiet escape the next morning. It was uncomfortable to say the least. I'd started asking him to go to the girl's home from now on and things have been much better. For me. I've heard rumors of how much girls are starting to hate him for disappearing in the morning, but that wasn't my problem.

"Of course." He smiled and hurried off to where I'm sure his new friend was waiting. He knew better than to leave too soon, but I doubted I'd see him again.

I sat with Emma and Ollie for the dinner but resumed my hostess responsibilities after the meal. I mingled with as many people as I could before I started getting tired. People were starting to trickle out, so I moved to the doors to give my thanks as they left.

A few of the players joined me, but Erik had disappeared, and so had Reese. I was disappointed he was the type to flake out. Especially as a new player. People needed to see his face and meet him if they were going to cheer for him.

I peeked into the ballroom and nearly burst out laughing. Reese was running around with the few children that were left. Their parents were sitting at tables talking amongst themselves while their kids chased Reese.

I moved into the room and leaned against the wall, trying to go unnoticed.

Reese had removed his suit coat and tie, making him look a lot more human. His sleeves were rolled to his elbows, exposing his thick forearms. He ran up behind a small boy and caught him. He tossed him in the air and caught him twice before setting him down. The boy's laugh filled the room, making it impossible not to smile.

This wasn't the same man who had been walking around the arena for the past week. He looked so relaxed. So happy. He wasn't doing this for show. Less than twenty people were left in the room and the cameras were long gone. This was the real Reese Murray.

A young girl ran up to him and froze. He looked down at

her with a wide smile and she screamed with delight as he chased her. I couldn't tell if they were playing tag or if there was a real direction for the game. It appeared the kids just wanted his attention and he was more than willing to give it to them.

I watched him drop to the ground on all fours and give rides to the remaining kids until he collapsed on the ground, his laughter filling the room. How he had the energy to run around with the kids was unfathomable.

He finally stood and gave each child a high five before walking back to his table and pulling on his coat. He was walking toward the doors now but hadn't noticed me. It wasn't until he was a few feet away that he looked up and met my eyes.

"Chloe? What are you still doing here?"

I smiled and nodded to where he'd been. "Just enjoying the show."

His grin was in full force. "They're fun."

"Do you have any nieces or nephews?"

He shook his head. "No. I'm an only child."

That was surprising. He'd been so good with them I'd assumed he either had little siblings or he was an uncle. "Oh."

He slipped his tie over his head and continued to watch me. "Can you leave or do you have to finish up here?"

Was he asking me to leave with him? No. He was just making conversation. But why?

"I need to check in with a few of the suppliers."

He nodded once. "Alright. Have a good night, Chloe."

"You too." I watched him walk out the doors and wished I was going with him.

But unlike my brother, I was crawling into bed alone before midnight.

8

REESE

Taking an elevator had never been so hard. A front office never filled me with anxiety. In Boston we were treated like kings. Here no one even looked up when the doors opened and I walked past cubicles.

I slid past the general manager's door, hoping he wouldn't notice me. I was on a mission and any deterrence might take away my courage.

I was finally there.

Nothing left to do but knock.

And risk whatever was on the other side.

Would she tear me apart? Would she be kind and funny like at the gala? The woman was a loose cannon.

Before I gained any suspicion from her coworkers, I knocked.

She called me in. She sounded fine. Happy maybe? Hopefully that wouldn't change when she saw me.

I watched her face and her smile never wavered. If she was disappointed, she didn't show it, but women were sneaky that way.

"Hi, Reese, what can I do for you?" Her voice was all business. Not that I was expecting anything else.

She hadn't invited me to sit but she hadn't kicked me out either.

I took my chances and pulled a chair away from her desk.

"I need your help." I broke the silence.

That got her attention she looked up from her computer with a worried expression.

"I'm not over PR."

That's what she thought of me? My first week on the team and I already needed someone to cover up a mistake. Great.

"No. It's nothing like that."

Her silence propelled me to continue.

"You said you'd help the other guys with their charities, right?"

She nodded. Woman of few words. How rare.

"I was wondering if you'd help me with mine."

She fell back in her chair and a slow smile emerged. "Tell me more."

That was all the encouragement I needed. "I started a foundation in Boston, but I asked a teammate to take it over. I want to start the same thing here."

She smiled, barely. "What kind of foundation?"

"I provide gear for children that otherwise wouldn't have the opportunity to learn to play hockey."

"Like jerseys?"

"Not just that. Stakes, pads, sticks, helmets, everything a kid would need."

"Boys and girls?"

"Yes."

Her smile grew.

54

"In Boston, I set up a league, so they could have practices and experience games. There were a few great things that worked well, but there are changes I'd like to make."

She turned in her seat and faced her computer. "Let's get started."

An hour later, I left her office feeling much more prepared than I'd ever been in Boston. She knew what she was doing, and she seemed to really believe in this cause. Almost all foundations and charity organizations have a good purpose, and I've seen teammates change people's lives with theirs. The difference with mine was that I hoped to impact one thousand kids a year, and those kids could turn around and teach a friend and so on. It was something I really believed in but having Chloe on my team made it so much sweeter.

She gave me homework to complete before our next meeting and cautioned me not to expect her to do all the work, which I would never do. Having an reason to see her again was all the motivation I needed. I didn't want to let her down, and I really didn't want to give her an excuse to go back to her first impression of me.

I wasn't a jerk, I'd just been having a bad day. Hopefully, after working together, she would realize that.

She was more than what I first thought too. She wasn't just the bossy woman that let the people around her expect her to do everything. It was almost an oxymoron.

I stood and paused in front of the door. "Does your offer still stand?"

She looked at me, obviously confused. "What offer?"

"The one to show me around town? I know that was for all the new guys, so I probably missed it."

A smile tugged at the corner of her mouth. "You did."

Great. Shut down with two words.

"But I'd be willing to put together a second session."

I narrowed my eyes. What was she getting at?

"I treat it as if I were a tour guide. I'd have to call a few places and see if I can get us in to see the capitol building and museum, but I can probably make it work. There are a few sites that are better to see during the day, but I'll make an exception."

She said it so frank I had to nod. Of course she did. She was all business all the time.

She cracked and began laughing. "I'm kidding. I took the guys out to dinner, told them where they would be safe eating without getting harassed by fans, and what areas to avoid."

I relaxed, just a bit. I couldn't read this woman.

"Tonight. You can pick me up."

"I don't have your address or number."

She smirked. "Ask one of the guys."

I narrowed my eyes. Asking for her number would be a death sentence. This was a test. It had to be.

"Sounds good. I'll see you tonight."

"Seven."

"I'll see you at seven." I opened the door and left before she could add any other terms. Like I needed to be dressed in a gorilla suit and speak in a Russian accent all night. Any other impossible or embarrassing task would tip me over the edge.

This had to be a joke. I stared at Hartman waiting for him to laugh, or smirk, or wink. Anything to tell me he was kidding.

"She lives with him?"

He nodded his head and pulled the strap of his duffle bag over his shoulder. "I'll text you the address. Maybe you'll get lucky and he won't be home."

I watched him leave the locker room before falling onto the closest bench. That sneaky little brat. She was doing this to me on purpose. She wouldn't have to go out with me if I was dead. And I was pretty sure I would be if I knocked on Erik's door and asked for his sister.

It would have been nice of her to warn me. Luckily, Hartman did. He was probably sitting in his Mercedes laughing all the way back to his house.

I could do this. I'd done harder things in my life. I made it to the NHL. Picking up a girl from her house was nothing.

I repeated that to myself at home as I got cleaned up and checked the clock. I needed to head over. To meet my doom.

Maybe he wouldn't be there. Maybe he wouldn't even care.

It's not like this was a date. She was showing me around, professionally.

I pulled into the parking lot in front of the building and cursed. I should just leave. Was a night with her worth my life?

Since when was I such a pansy?

I got out of my car and walked through the doors. A man in uniform greeted me.

"Hi, I'm here for Chloe Schultz."

He nodded. "She let me know she was expecting you. Use the elevators on the left. Floor twenty-five."

No unnecessary small talk. I liked him. "Thank you."

I wiped my hands on my pants while the elevator rose. I felt like a teenager again. Next thing would be me breaking out in pimples and my voice would be an octave higher.

The doors opened and I stepped out. There were only

two doors, but I didn't know which one to use. The doorman hadn't specified, and Hartman hadn't given me the specifics. I was on the verge of flipping a coin when the door to the right opened.

Erik glared at me.

"I thought I heard the elevator ding."

"Hey. I…" I don't know what to say. I'm here for your sister? I'm here on business? Please don't kill me now or later on the ice.

"You're here to see Chloe?"

I nodded. This guy had never intimidated me before, but now I felt like I was meeting a girl's father. The kind that clean their guns in front of guys like me.

"She told me you were going out tonight."

I nodded again like the idiot I was.

He eyed me like he was sizing me up. I was a bit bigger than him, but he had that territorial thing going for him.

"Don't hurt her."

That wasn't what I'd been expecting.

"I won't."

He stepped into the hall and closed the door behind him. "I don't think you understand. The team is my life. It's Chloe's life. She will do anything for anyone in the organization, and guys have taken advantage of that in the past."

I wanted to ask who, but I doubted he'd tell me.

"They aren't around anymore."

His expression cleared up any question I had about why they were gone. He got rid of them. Poor guys.

"You're not the first guy to look at her and see an easy target."

"Erik." I had to stop him. I wouldn't let him think of me like that. "That's not it at all."

He smirked. "Then what is it?"

"I'm new to the city. She offered to show me around. That's it."

He shook his head. "You're an even bigger idiot than I thought if you won't admit it to yourself."

I tried to defend myself, but he put a hand on my shoulder and leveled me with a glare. "Don't hurt her. If you're attracted to her, fine. If you want to spend time with her, fine. If you think you have a chance at dating her, you're wrong, but fine. One wrong move and you're done."

He was serious, and I respected him for it.

"You have my word."

He nodded and stepped back. "I'll let her know you're here."

He stepped back into the apartment and shut the door in my face. I guess I wasn't invited in. Yet.

I only waited a minute or two before the door opened again and the much nicer, more attractive Schultz appeared.

"Hi." She looked beautiful in a simple cotton dress and sandals. Her hair was loose around her shoulders and I couldn't help but smile. "Sorry I didn't get to the door first. I was trying to listen for you, but Erik beat me to it."

"No worries." I pressed the button to call the elevator. "You look great."

"Thanks." She didn't look uncomfortable at my compliment. Most women would have downplayed it or blushed. Chloe just accepted it with a smile. Like she knew it.

Once we were in my car I turned it on and waited. "Where to first?"

She ignored me and pushed the buttons to find the radio and found a station that played pop music. I guess she felt at home with me.

"We're going to drive around for a bit, so you can get familiar with where things are. If you have any questions or want to see anything specific let me know. Then we'll get dinner."

"Sounds good." She seemed to have this plan down, so I let her direct me down the road.

"Where are you from, Reese Murray?"

I eyed her. She really hadn't looked me up?

"Michigan."

"And you're an only child."

She remembered. That didn't mean anything. It was her job to know about the players. "Yeah. Are you going to ask my favorite color next?"

She laughed. "No. I already know."

"What? How?"

She laughed harder. "It's black and red."

I rolled my eyes. "I'm not allowed to like colors that aren't on our jersey?"

"You can like them, but your loyalty needs to be to the black and red."

I glanced over to see her smiling at me. "Yes, Coach."

"Consider yourself lucky that I'm not."

"Oh yeah? You think you could do his job?"

She smacked my arm. "I've been watching hockey since I was three. I know the ins and outs. I can spot weaknesses in a player that they've never known. I know the plays as well as Erik. Nothing against Coach Romney, he's amazing, but I could do it."

She was sure. I had no reason to doubt her. "Good to know we have backup if we need it."

She laughed again. "I always wanted to do a twin swap back when we were kids. I wanted to prove to Erik I could play as well as him, but he never went for it."

"He probably didn't want to prove you right."

I looked over at her as she shrugged. "Probably."

"Did you ever play?"

"No." She sighed. "My mom thought it was too dangerous for me."

"But not Erik?"

"Nope."

"That's quite the double standard."

"Oh, I know. I fought her about it constantly, but eventually I got over it. Erik had to work really hard and I was more interested in playing with my friends. I got to have sleepovers and go to the movies, but Erik was always at the rink."

I knew exactly what she meant. "My friends didn't understand why I couldn't play after school. They thought I didn't like them, but I was always at practice."

"It takes a lifetime of dedication to get to where you guys are."

It did, and it was refreshing to be around someone who understood that. Every girl in high school and college ended up breaking up with me because they said I didn't give them enough attention. I never tried to ignore them, but I was busy. Between classes, homework, practice, and games, I barely had time to sleep. I didn't have to explain that to Chloe, though.

She raised her arm and pointed. "Turn here."

We drove through the downtown area where the arena was located. I'd managed to find an apartment a few blocks away, which was near where she lived.

"Down this road is an outdoor shopping area."

I nodded as if that interested me.

"Turn left at the light."

I followed her instructions as we drove farther from the arena.

"There's the convention center. Down that road are two theaters. I'm not sure if you're into that."

"Actually..." I smiled and turned down the street to where she pointed. "I've been wanting to see where that was."

"Really?" Her surprise wasn't completely unwarranted. I wasn't necessarily a fan of the theater, but if it made her happy I was willing to pretend.

I stopped the car in front where the marquee was lit with *The Founders'* sign.

"What are you doing?"

I pointed the to the entrance. "Have you seen it?"

She shook her head. "I wish."

This had worked out better than I could have imagined. I planned on giving her the tickets at the office, but this was perfect.

"Well, that's good."

She chuckled. "Not for me."

I opened the center console and pulled out an envelope.

"But it is for me."

I handed her the envelope and watched as she took it. She looked at me with narrowed eyes and broke the seal. She pulled out the two tickets and shrieked.

"Reese! How?"

She looked from her lap to me, grinning like I'd just given her the world.

"I heard you hadn't had a chance to see it, so I used my connections."

"Thank you!" She threw her arms around me and squeezed. It took me a moment to respond. I wrapped my arms around her slim shoulders. This was the closest we'd ever been and I wanted it to last as long as possible. Her sweet scent was overwhelming, intoxicating.

"I hope you enjoy it."

She leaned back. "I will." She paused and looked down

at the tickets. "Thank you so much. I don't know how I'll ever repay you."

I shook my head. "I don't want you to. I just wanted to make up for the problems I've caused. I promise I'm not normally as *gruff* as I've been lately."

She smirked. "Sorry about that."

I laughed. "I deserved it."

I merged back onto the street. "Now where?"

We drove around for another hour. She covered everything. The best grocery stores. The best gas station to use without being hounded by fans. Touristy places to avoid. The best restaurants. Even though I knew she'd gone through this with almost every other guy on the team, she made it feel personal.

"Any questions?"

"You mentioned dinner." I'd appreciated her taking the time to show me everything, but my stomach was growling. I wasn't used to waiting so long to eat.

She smiled. "Sorry. Turn left on the next street."

Minutes later we pulled into a parking lot in front of a Mexican restaurant, Los Gatos.

"The cats?" I chuckled as we walked in.

She laughed with me. "The owner is a past player. He let the team name it when he opened it. They voted and thought this was the funniest name."

"That was brave of him." I opened the door and waited for her to walk in.

"Phil is pretty laid back. He didn't care about the name, just the food."

The hostess greeted Chloe by name. "I'll take you back." She smiled briefly at me. It was nice to be treated like a normal person. No staring or giggling. She must be used to athletes if the owner was a past player.

I was wrong.

She wasn't fazed because the back room was packed with almost the entire team.

I glanced at Chloe, but she was already walking to two open spaces at a nearly full table. Erik and Hartman nodded a greeting when I took the seat across from her. A few of the players yelled hello to us. She brought me into the lion's den and judging by the guys' reactions to her being there they expected her.

"Is this a regular thing?" I asked with an even tone. I didn't want her or anyone else to know how uncomfortable I was.

She hid behind her menu. Coward.

Erik answered for her. Shocker.

"We come almost every Tuesday. Unless there's a game."

9

CHLOE

I listened to their conversation from behind the menu like a coward. I just wanted Reese to see that the team was on his side.

"That must mean it's good." Reese sounded a bit more relaxed after Erik spoke to him without threatening injury. My brother is a bit rough around the edges when he first meets people, but it's just his way of protecting himself. He isn't the type to let people in.

"It's the best in the city. Phil's done a great job."

I peeked up and nearly sighed when I saw them sharing chips and salsa. No one would fight over that. It would be un-American.

A waitress came to take our order, and Erik even made suggestions for Reese. See, they could play nicely.

"Will I get to meet Phil?" Reese asked Erik, then noticed me staring.

"I'll go see if he's around." I shot up and hurried out of the room. I had a feeling Reese would make me pay for bringing him here and leaving him alone, but he was a big boy. He needed to feel like he was a part of the team, and fast. The first game was next week.

I peeked into the kitchen and saw Phil at the window, shuffling plates.

"Hey."

He turned to me and smiled. "Hi, Chloe. I should have known you'd show up at some point." He walked over and wrapped me in a bear hug.

He'd retired from the team when I was a child, but he was still considered an honorary member. It was a bit unusual for a former player to stay around, but he said this city was his home, and Canada was too cold, so we were stuck with him.

"I was showing a new player around."

"I heard."

Of course he had. The team gossiped more than a group of school girls.

"He's in the back room with the rest of them if you want to meet him." He led the way back and immediately introduced himself to Reese.

If there was anyone who could make someone feel comfortable, it was Phil. He was my pseudo dad, although most of the team felt that way.

"It's nice to meet you, Reese. I've watched you for the past few years. The Fury is lucky to have you."

I stole a glance at Erik to gauge his reaction, but he didn't reveal anything. It wasn't something most people would argue. Reese was an excellent player, and as long as they learned how to work together, he and Erik would be unstoppable.

"Thank you. I'm glad to be here."

He was? I looked at him and he smiled back at me.

Maybe he was getting over being traded. That was the first step to getting on the team's good side. Be grateful and excited to be here.

Two waiters walked in carrying trays of food. "I better get back to the kitchen to make sure all you guys get fed. I'll see you all later."

I returned to my seat and remained quiet. Reese resumed a conversation with Hartman and Olli. This was just what they needed. I had to resist the urge to pat myself on the back. Reese needed a few days to adjust and the team needed a chance to get to know him.

Mission accomplished.

I should have known the peace would be short-lived.

I brought my laptop with me to work during practice the next day. The Pride was sitting around me talking and watching the guys. I was writing an article about the gala when Sasha shook my shoulder.

"What?" I looked over at her, but she was pointing to the ice.

Erik and Reese were staring each other down, just inches from each other. I couldn't hear what they were saying but I guessed by their expressions they weren't exchanging pleasantries.

I stood, but Sasha pulled me down. "You can't get involved. Whatever is going on between those two needs to be settled by them."

I closed my laptop and watched. "They were fine last night."

She scooted closer to me and leaned in. "Porter

mentioned this morning that some of the guys were saying Erik threatened Reese when you weren't around. I guess they only played nice in front of you."

Why didn't that surprise me? "What did Erik say?"

"That you were off limits and to stay away from you."

I fought the urge to run onto the ice and fight my brother myself. "Why does he feel the need to do that? I haven't had a date in three years because of him."

Sasha gasped. "Oh, honey." She rubbed my arm with a look of genuine concern.

"He's been threatening guys since we were twelve. I'm a grown woman and can spend time with whomever I wish."

Her lips turned up. "Now that's what I like to hear. It's about time you stood up to him."

"What?"

"Oh, don't get mad. I've just watched him dictate your life since you guys moved here. I've been waiting for you to get fed up and tell him to back off."

We've been here for four years. She's been waiting for me to get my crap together for that long?

"Why didn't you say anything?"

"It wasn't my place. He's the only family you have. I wasn't going to try to mess with your dynamics. I knew you'd figure it out yourself...eventually."

I sighed and leaned into her.

"Granted, I thought it would have happened a lot sooner, but we all do things in our own time." She patted my head like a child, and suddenly I felt like one.

I was sick of Erik bossing me around, even if it was indirectly. I could make my own decisions.

"Oh, Chloe." I turned and three of the women behind me pointed to a woman walking down the stairs a few sections away.

Great. I was not in the mood for this.

I stood and marched down the row where I intercepted the intruder.

"Can I help you?"

She looked at me and smiled. "I'm just here to watch."

I looked her over. She didn't strike me as a reporter. I knew most of them anyway.

"This is a closed practice."

Her smile faded. "Oh well." She looked to the ice. "I was invited."

"By?"

She crossed her arms defiantly. "A new guy."

I smirked. "Does he have a name?"

She glanced away again. "Murray?"

I had to bite my cheek to keep from laughing. Reese was currently in the corner closest to us. His jersey was the easiest to read.

"What's his first name?"

She tilted her head. "Why does it matter to you if I'm here?"

"Because these practices aren't open to the public. I'm going to have to ask you to leave."

"You have no right."

Oh, honey. I looked up the stairs to the security guard and nodded.

"I do actually. You can either leave now on your own, or I'll have my friend Rob escort you."

She looked over her shoulder. Rob was halfway down the steps.

"What's your problem?"

"Right now? It's you."

"You're such a b—."

"Alright, ma'am. Time to go." Rob took her elbow and led her up the steps.

I watched her leave and let out a frustrated breath. What was with people's attitude? They were trespassing, yet I was the one in the wrong.

When I got back to the Pride, I didn't bother trying to work again. I was too distracted.

"Good job, girl."

"You showed her."

I acknowledged the comments with a wave but kept my eyes on the ice. Emma left me alone, giving my shoulder a squeeze when she left.

Instead of heading back up to my office when practice ended, I waited. I sat on a foldout chair outside the locker room so there was no chance he could slip away from me.

I greeted the other players as they trickled out. None of them seemed surprised to see me there. They probably knew what the fight was about. I debated asking Hartman when he left, but he just shook his head and passed me. Even the captain was over the fighting.

When Erik walked out, I remained in my spot and waited for him to see me. He was almost in front of me when he looked up from his phone and paused.

"What?" Oh good, he was in an even worse mood than I was.

I stood and looked up at him. He might have six inches on me, but I wasn't going to let him intimidate me. "We need to talk."

He sighed and threw his head back. "Later." He pushed past me, but I caught his arm.

"No, we need to talk now."

He looked down at me with narrowed eyes. "Outside."

I followed him through the tunnels until we were into the parking structure. Most of the team and front office parked here, so it wasn't exactly private, but I wasn't willing to wait until I got home.

"What was that about?" Erik looked at me like I was speaking a foreign language. "The fight. What was it about?"

"Nothing."

"You got into a fight during practice, Erik. With a teammate." I attempted to keep my voice level, but he wasn't just making me angry, he was scaring me. This wasn't who he was. He'd never had a problem with another player before. What about Reese was driving him so crazy?

"It was nothing." He turned to leave but I stopped him. I moved around him to face him.

"It wasn't nothing, Erik. You've been a different person since Reese got here. You've been rude and mean and completely irrational."

His stare should have melted me. "You don't get it."

"No, I don't. Explain it to me." I hated feeling like there was something between us. We'd always gotten along. We were two halves to a whole.

"Reese..." He sighed and glared over my shoulder. "He's..."

I stayed silent while he worked through his own thoughts.

"You need to stay away from him."

"What?"

"I don't want you going near him. Just stay away, Chloe."

"Excuse me?"

There was a flash of guilt in his eyes before he turned back to stone.

"You don't get to dictate who I do or do not spend time

with. You don't get to fight people because of me. I'm a grown woman. I can make my own decisions."

He glared at me, but there was no way his anger matched mine.

"I'm done, Erik." I stepped back and turned back to the tunnel.

"What's that supposed to mean?"

I spun around. "I'm moving out. I'm not going to let you keep controlling me."

His façade cracked. "No. You don't have to do that."

"I think I do. It's time."

He shook his head. "Chloe, you're being dramatic. You don't need to move out."

"If I don't, nothing will change."

He sighed and rolled his shoulders. "I won't get into any more fights."

"And?"

His jaw flexed. "I won't tell you who to see."

"And?"

He looked confused. "What else?"

"You need to give me space. I need to live life on my terms." I paused. Maybe he needed the space just as much as me. "I can't always be around for you. You need to be able to live on your own as well."

The look on his face reminded me so much of our father I almost cried.

"I'll try."

"That's all I can ask."

He nodded and walked toward me. He hugged me so tightly I was sure he'd popped my back. "I'm not ready to lose you."

I wrapped my arms around his torso. "You'll never lose me."

He mumbled something into my hair, but I couldn't understand it. He released me and stepped back. "Get back to work. I'll see you tonight."

It may not have been a total victory, but I hoped he'd really heard me. I wasn't going to tolerate it anymore.

10

REESE

Hartman was sitting by my locker when I walked in for practice. At least it wasn't Coach. That would have meant trouble. Though judging by his expression he wasn't about to go easy on me. I was hoping he would have cooled off overnight.

He looked up casually and watched me as I dropped my duffle and sat across from him. I wasn't going to be the one to speak first. I'd learn as a kid not to offer any information. Always let them lead the conversation.

"This needs to stop."

His voice was calm, but I could tell he was holding something back.

"I'm not trying—"

"No. You're not. Whatever chip is living on your shoulder needs to go. I know how hard being traded is. I understand, but you need to let that go."

"I have."

He narrowed his eyes. "Have you?"

I nodded. "Yeah. It was a shock for the first few days, but I adjusted."

"Then what's going on?"

We were alone. Even though he and Erik were friends, I knew he put his title of captain first.

"Erik has been making threats since the day I started."

"I don't understand why. He's never been like this before. He's the type to be friends with everyone."

Had anyone else displayed an interest in his sister? I doubted anyone had been stupid enough. Until me.

"I don't think he appreciates me spending time with his sister."

Hartman sighed and leaned back. "Is that what this is all about? You're fighting over Chloe?"

"Don't say it like that."

"Like what, Murray? There's a million women in this city. Why her?"

This was my captain. I couldn't punch him. I took a deep breath and tried to remain calm. "She's not just some girl. She's amazing. She's selfless and accepting. She gets what it's like—"

"Stop. You're going down a path you don't want to be on."

I tried to argue but he held his hand up. "That's his sister, Murray. His twin. They are all each other has. They've been through hell and back together."

His expression darkened. What had they gone through? "What happened?"

He rubbed his face with his hand. "It's not my place to tell you, but you'll just look it up after I leave." He sighed. "Their parents were killed in an accident when they were in high school. It was right before their graduation. Chloe changed her plans and went to school near Erik so they wouldn't be apart. They haven't left each other since."

I knew they were close, closer than normal siblings, but now I understood.

"He's protective of her. A little too much, but that's between them."

"I get it."

He leaned forward. "I know she's gorgeous and as sweet as they come, but you need to let whatever you may have thought or felt go. For the sake of the team."

I opened my mouth, but he held up a hand.

"You won't be the first person to sacrifice their feelings for the good of the season, Murray. I'm not saying you need to avoid her. She's a part of this team. She's family. So, treat her that way. She's your sister right now. Maybe over the summer you can pursue her, but I need your head clear and I need you and Schultz to work together. I need my first line solid and that won't happen if there's drama happening off the ice."

I didn't like being told what to do, but he was right.

"I don't date during the season anyway."

"That's a good rule to have." He smirked. "I don't date while I'm in the NHL but whatever works best for you."

I laughed, then noticed his expression hadn't changed. "You're serious?"

"You don't get to be the captain of a championship team by worrying about women and relationships."

I couldn't argue with that. He was the best in the league, and that required complete focus.

My respect for him increased. Not only did he call me out without making a scene, but he put the team first.

"I'll clear things up with Schultz before practice."

He stood and patted my shoulder twice before leaving.

I changed and was pulling on my pads when Erik finally

walked in. He glanced at me before turning and walking to his locker on the opposite side of the room.

Once I was laced up I stood, nodded to the other guys getting ready, and stopped in front of him.

"The team comes first."

He looked up at me. "Yeah?"

"I'm willing to put everything that's happened behind us. Start over."

He looked away for a second before nodding. "Fine."

That had been easier than I'd thought. I was about to turn when he grabbed my wrist. "You stay away from her though."

I looked where his hand was cutting off circulation to my fingers then back to his eyes. "Fine."

He dropped his hand.

"For now."

I walked away before he could respond and got out onto the ice. I did a few laps to warm up while waiting for everyone else to come out. I could feel eyes on me and Schultz as we ran drills, then a short game. We played nice, though, so there wasn't much of a show to watch. He and I actually worked well together.

By the time Coach blew the last whistle, the team was staring at us. "That's enough, ladies. My eyes are up here."

We all turned to him and waited.

"Tomorrow is the event at the hospital. I expect everyone there in jerseys by ten a.m."

There were a few grumbles, but we couldn't really complain about visiting sick children without looking like complete jerks.

"See you guys tomorrow."

He waved us off the ice, not that we had to be told twice.

There was nothing that sounded better than a shower at that moment. Until I looked into the stands. Chloe was sitting a few rows up. Staring at me. When she realized I was watching her, she looked down to her laptop. I waited for a few seconds, but she was determined to ignore me. It was probably for the best.

I went back to stretch and change before leaving for the day. Normally I would have gone straight for my car, but I was curious. Was she still there? I walked to the end of the tunnel and looked across the ice.

There she was.

Alone.

She was looking down at her computer, so she was probably working. Hopefully writing a better post about me.

I should leave.

Hartman warned me.

I needed to keep my head in the game. Focus on what was important.

I knew that. But my feet were carrying me toward her. I walked down the row, wrapping around two corners until I was closing in on her.

She didn't look up until I was sitting next to her.

"What are you doing?" Her shocked expression made me laugh.

"Seeing if you're writing a retraction for my previous bio."

She smirked. "You don't read the team blog? I'm hurt."

"What do you mean?"

"I changed it a while ago. I believe it may have been the night you gave me the tickets." She winked.

Huh. I should take a look at the website more often.

"What brings you to my office today?" She closed her laptop and looked at me.

"I was just wondering what the view is like from up here. You seem to like it."

She looked around. "It's the center."

I nodded. "But you don't like sitting against the glass?" Those were the expensive seats. Fans loved sitting up next to the action.

"I like this vantage point. It allows me to see things from a different perspective from the players."

"And that's a good thing?"

She shrugged. "I've been able to point some things out to Erik and the guys in the past."

Of course she had.

"You'll have to let me know if you see anything I can improve on."

She turned to me. "You need to trust your line."

That caught me off guard. "What?"

She stared into my eyes like she was searching my soul. "You hesitate when you pass."

No, I didn't. Did I? I looked away, breaking the contact.

"You didn't do that in Boston."

She's been watching my film?

"Stalker?" I laughed trying to lighten the mood. I wasn't used to receiving criticizing from someone that didn't play the game.

"I'm just trying to help." I looked back at her and she seemed resigned.

"I know. I'm sorry. What do I need to do?"

Her eyes dropped to my lips.

Or did they?

"You don't trust them to be where they're supposed to. You wait to see them before passing and it gives away your move. They'll be where you need them to be. You knew that with your old team." She shrugged. "Maybe it's something that comes with time, but that's something I've noticed."

I didn't want to admit to her that she was right. It was second nature in Boston. I could predict exactly where my teammates would be. I could anticipate their moves. I hadn't developed that with Erik and Hartman yet.

"I'll work on it." She smiled, just barely. A strand of hair was in her face and I wanted so badly to reach out and brush it away. I wanted to touch her smooth skin. Pull her in. Kiss her.

"Chloe?"

A voice from above broke the moment.

I looked up to see her assistant standing at the top of the bowl with her hands on her hips.

"I've got to go." Her voice rasped. She stood and hurried up the steps before I could stop her.

Had she felt that? There was something between us. I swear it. Hartman's warning played in my mind. This was a bad idea. A terrible idea. One that would get me in trouble with the team. But that wasn't stopping me from planning a way to see her again.

11

CHLOE

I wouldn't be able to avoid him forever. Not even for a few hours. It was the first time in my career I regretted my job. If I hadn't asked to be over events I wouldn't be here actively avoiding Reese.

All of the guys were lined up for a few photos with the administration of the hospital, so I was on the opposite side of the room pretending to be very busy with making sure each child on the three floors we were covering would have a visitor.

I'd made this schedule three weeks ago. I knew it backward and forward. It was fine, but I needed a seemingly valid excuse for being away from the action.

One of the photographers covering the event walked up to me. "Chloe, do you know where I'm stationed?"

"Yes." I flipped a page back. "John, you are level four, rooms 400 through 410."

"Thanks. I'll see you later."

I waved, then resumed my hiding. Kristen was eyeing me from the corner where she was giving directions to other photographers. She knew something was up. I was usually front row center for these things. Now I had two people I had to avoid.

The team broke formation and began milling around awaiting direction. Crap. This was me.

You can do this.

"Alright, Furies. I need your attention."

Within seconds the room was silent. Good, they still feared me. At least in my head they did.

"I have your room assignments. Please hit all of these before wandering around. I want to make sure every child gets a visit. After you've gone to your rooms, you can go visit your friends."

I looked to Hartman and he smirked. He'd been coming here for so long on his own he was on a first name basis will all of the nurses and the long-term patients. It might seem heartless to give out assignments, but there were a lot of kids to see and I didn't want anyone missed.

"Yes, ma'am."

"Good. I know we have some fans here, so if a kid you visit mentions his favorite player is someone other than you, let me know so I can try to get him there."

I watched for nods before continuing. "Please see me or Kristen before leaving to get your assignments."

I hurried through the line that gathered in front of me until there was only one person waiting.

"Reese."

He stepped forward. "Where am I going?"

I looked down to my papers even though I already knew. "Fifth floor, rooms 530 through 540."

"Thanks." He didn't leave. He just stared down at me.

"Reese." I took a breath. "I think we should keep our distance today."

I looked around at the cameras ready to snap a picture

82

of a player and front office employee in a compromising position.

He didn't look surprised. "I'll see you later."

I watched him walk to the elevator until the doors closed. I needed to keep a clear head today. I couldn't, no, *wouldn't*, be distracted by a dumb, handsome, confusing player.

Kristen and I walked the halls, making ourselves available for questions.

"Why are you so on edge today?"

I wanted to ignore the question, but she'd never let me.

"I just want everything to be perfect."

"It will be. It always is." When I didn't reply, she stopped and tugged my wrist to get me to face her. "This wouldn't have anything to do with a certain player would it?"

"I don't know what you're talking about."

She rolled her eyes. "Please. You two can't be in the same room without making gaga eyes at each other."

"That's not true."

She ignored me. "You can fight it all you want but there's definitely something between you two."

She thought so? Maybe I wasn't as crazy as I'd convinced myself. "There can't be anything."

She smirked. "Why not?"

I looked down at my clipboard, wishing there was some emergency I could run off to. "The season is about to start."

"So?"

"I don't date players." She knew that. Everyone knew it.

She laughed and tugged on my elbow. "We both know that wasn't going to hold up forever. You're surrounded by them. They're the only guys you know. Of course you're going to end up with one."

I rolled my eyes. "Erik isn't okay with it."

She hit me with her clipboard. "Erik is a big boy who can get over it."

I stepped back and hit the elevator button. "It's a bad idea. It's better that we're just friends right now."

She shook her head. "Honey, that man is not interested in friendship with you."

I ignored her and walked into the elevator. We had one more floor to check.

She huffed but joined me.

I peeked into a few rooms and smiled at the guys hanging out with kids. They were so happy. I knew they looked forward to this day each year, the kids and the team.

We reached the nurses' station, which was surprisingly empty. Except for one blonde nurse. She was leaning against the counter laughing at someone. I walked forward until I could see.

Reese.

The nurse laughed again, putting her hands on his chest and leaving them there a little too long.

I stepped forward until Reese saw me. His eyes widened as mine narrowed. "Sorry to break this up, but you have sick children to visit on the fourth floor, Mr. Murray. They asked for you."

The nurse was smart enough to drop her hands and look a tiny bit guilty. Until she grabbed a card out of her pocket and stuck it in Reese's pocket. His back pocket.

"Call me."

He smiled at the bimbo before walking past me and a suspiciously quiet Kristen.

We got back on the elevator, riding in silence. When the doors opened, Reese didn't bother looking at me.

"What are the room numbers?"

"404 and 431."

He walked away without another word.

"Yeah, there's no chance of friendship with that man, Chloe."

I turned and glared at Kristen, but she just shrugged and walked away.

12

REESE

S he had no right to get mad.

She just told me to keep my distance.

Now she thought she could judge me for talking to another woman?

Speak of the devil. I walked out of the last room feeling emotionally spent and way too aggravated from spending the day with some of the best people I'd ever met dealing with some of the very worst circumstances and there she was.

I needed to make things clear. She couldn't have it both ways.

I waited until she was alone before approaching. Unlike her, I knew how to be polite instead of losing my head. She was looking down at a stack of papers until I was right in front of her.

She looked up with a surprised expression.

"We need to talk."

She didn't argue so I led her to an empty room and closed the door behind her.

She turned to face me but said nothing. Her calmness

irritated me. How could she stand there like nothing was wrong? Like she hadn't just embarrassed herself, and me, in front of the nurse. I took a breath to calm down.

"You can't have it both ways, Chloe. You can't push me away then get upset when I speak to someone else." I fought to keep my voice level. I wanted to yell but knew she wouldn't react well to that.

"I'm not mad you were talking to her. I'm upset that you're wasting time when you could be visiting children."

Big fat lie.

"You're lying." She didn't argue. Her self-righteous attitude needed to go. She was in the wrong and I knew she just didn't want to admit it. "You told me to keep my distance, and I was. You have nothing to get upset over."

I was hurting her. I could see it in her eyes. But I was doing what was right. What needed to happen. That didn't mean my heart agreed, though.

"Besides, it's not like I was going to ask her out. I don't date during the season."

"I don't date players." It was her only defense and I was ready for it.

"What does that have to do with me talking to the nurse?" I tried to stop myself from smiling but failed.

She narrowed her eyes. "I was just making sure we were both clear with where we stood."

I nodded. She was nervous. I was making her nervous. "Okay."

"Okay." She folded her arms and stared me down.

I clenched my jaw then released over and over again. She had something else to say, and I could wait her out. I could even prod a little.

"I spoke with your brother." Huh. Was that fear in her eyes? What was she hiding? "We agreed to start over."

She looked only slightly relieved.

"It's better for the team."

I tried to look into her eyes, but she turned away. She nodded like she agreed, but she didn't even know what she was agreeing to. She was so stubborn.

"It's better that we're just friends."

Her eyebrows pinched together in a scowl.

I nearly smiled. "We had one great date, but that can't happen again."

"Huh?" Her confusion quickly changed to defiance.

"The night we went out. You showed me the city? We had dinner." I had to bite the inside of my cheek to keep from smiling. She was getting so worked up.

"That wasn't a date." She nearly growled the words as she stepped toward me. Was she supposed to be threatening?

I shouldn't enjoy getting her riled up, but it was a little entertaining to see her try to intimidate me. "Wasn't it?"

"No." Her hands went to her hips. "I do that for all the guys."

"Alone?" I smirked to keep from laughing.

"Well, no, but you missed the first one."

"So, our conversation. That's standard for all of the guys?"

It hadn't been standard for me. I didn't go around telling the women my innermost thoughts, especially when I knew they had the power to use it against me. That was the trouble with Chloe. She had the power to destroy me. Not just my career, but my heart.

I needed to take that power back.

I stepped closer and tilted my head down, closer to her. "It can't happen again, Chloe."

Her breath caught when I said her name.

"No, it can't."

I leaned in until I could feel the heat of her skin, so close to my lips. I waited a beat to see if she would react, but she was frozen in place. "Goodbye then."

Before she had a chance to reply, I turned and left the room. I wanted to stay. I wanted to know if she felt the fire that ignited whenever we were close. We could both lie through our teeth that there was nothing between us, but that didn't make it true.

Neither of us wanted to open up. Neither of us was willing to get hurt, so of course we both were now.

I left the hospital without speaking to anyone. I couldn't handle being in there. I did the best I could with the children, but it was heartbreaking. I smiled and laughed and joked with them, but all I wanted to do was help them. I couldn't though. They were receiving the best care possible, I knew, but I wished I could take away their suffering. It wasn't fair.

Neither was Chloe's double standard.

The nurse was a fan. I was treating her like one.

Would Chloe rather I ignored the woman? Was I supposed to walk away when she asked for an autograph? Yeah. That would have been great publicity for the team.

It wasn't like I was asking her out. I was being courteous. A good representative for the Fury. I didn't deserve to be attacked for that.

I could speak to whomever I wanted. Chloe had turned me down. She was the one that told me to keep my distance. I was just following her wishes.

I pulled into my parking garage and slammed my hand against the steering wheel.

I couldn't win with that woman.

She wanted conflicting things and she expected me to live up to them.

When I got to my apartment I went to my room and changed into running clothes. There was only one way I was going to get over this and it was by working out. I couldn't go back to the arena. That would add gas to the fire in me, so running outside would have to do.

The first time my sole hit the concrete my shoulders relaxed. This was my therapy. I turned up my music and pushed out all thoughts.

13

CHLOE

I slammed the door behind me, not caring if the neighbors got mad. I dropped my purse on the floor, kicked off my heels, and threw myself face first on the couch. It wasn't enough. I grabbed a throw pillow and pulled it over my face, then screamed for as long as I could.

I felt better. Sometimes a girl just needed to completely lose it.

"Um...Chloe? You alright?"

Crap.

I dropped the pillow and rolled onto my stomach. "Oh hi. I didn't know you were home."

Erik was looking at me like I was insane, which wasn't that farfetched. "What's going on?"

I looked at the pillow and shrugged. "Sometimes you just have to let it out, ya know?"

He shook his head. "Not really."

Of course he didn't. Erik had always done what he wanted. Not that it was necessarily a bad thing, but he didn't have the same guilt I dealt with. He didn't think of what bad things could happen. He saw a goal and went for it.

I was the one left behind to deal with the aftermath. The crying girls he never called back. The press releases about his behavior at an event. The apologies for him not caring or not showing up to something.

"Maybe one day you will."

He stepped forward toward the kitchen before stopping. "What's that supposed to mean?"

"Nothing."

He folded his arms and gave me a serious look, the one that made him look just like Dad.

"You've never had to sacrifice anything. You've never had to make the hard choice. Putting something before your own desires."

You would have thought I just accused him of murder by his expression.

"You have no idea what you're talking about."

"Oh really? You got every lesson, private trainer, and new piece of equipment you asked for. Mom and Dad put you on that traveling team in middle school because you said you needed the experience. You told them real players started that way. But what you missed while you were traveling through the entire country and Canada was everything we had to sacrifice to make that dream possible for you. You didn't see Dad working two jobs. Mom taking extra shifts at the hospital. I was home alone from the moment I woke up until I went to bed. I raised myself because you needed to join that stupid team."

He tried to interrupt me but now that I'd lifted a corner of the box I'd been holding this in, the whole thing needed to be emptied.

"You didn't even notice when you were home. You asked them to fly you to see different agents because you said that was the next step. They took out a second mortgage to pay for that and the major junior league. You couldn't play for a local team. Oh no! You just had to play for the Seattle team. Where did you think they were getting this money the whole time? Did you ever stop for a second and think about that? No. You didn't. Do you know what I got to do while you were off living the dream? I got my first job at fourteen. Not because it was fun. Because I overheard Dad telling Mom he hadn't been eating lunch or dinner to save money. For three years, Erik. Dad sacrificed himself for you."

I looked into his eyes waiting to see if anything was sinking in, but he was turned away from me looking out the window.

"When they died there was so much debt. Did you ever think about how everything got taken care of? Did you ever wonder why I moved in with the neighbor? We lost the house. We lost everything, but you were too busy focusing on yourself to notice my world was falling apart. I gave up Yale not just because I wanted to be close to you, but because I couldn't afford it."

"What do you want me to say, Chloe?" I couldn't just hear it in his voice, but I could see that he felt dejected in his body. He looked weighed down. He looked how I felt every day. "I can't apologize for the past. Was I selfish? Yes. Was I completely self-absorbed? Definitely. No, I didn't know what was going on because Mom and Dad kept it from me. As a matter of fact, I don't remember *you* ever telling me either. Don't you think I would have quit and come straight home if I'd known how bad things were?"

I shook my head. I really didn't think he would have ever given up.

"You act like everything is your responsibility. You always have. You take the burden on yourself and you survive. You fix. But no one ever asked you to. If you had asked me to come home to help I would have. You don't get to hang this over me if I didn't know."

I hated that he was a little bit right.

"But in all the time you've spent stewing about this, and it's apparent you've spent years, have you ever stopped to think about it from my perspective?"

He thought he could justify himself?

"I got calls from all three of you at least once a week. I asked Mom and Dad how things were going. I asked about their jobs, the house, their cars. I worried about them every day I was gone. I asked how you were doing. If they had given me one tiny thread of evidence something was wrong I would have been home the next day."

He sighed and shook his head.

"Yes, I was off following my dream, but I was doing it because I was good. Because I'd been told by people over and over again that if I worked hard I could get here. Get to the NHL. So, I fought, and I worked, and I did everything I could to get here. But I wasn't just thinking of me. I was doing it for Mom and for Dad. I wanted to get here, in the NHL, as soon as I could so I could buy them their dream house in the mountains. I wanted to set them up so they could retire and never have to work again. I did this so you would never have to worry about money. I did this so we, you and me, could have the best possible future. So, don't sit there on your pedestal and tell me I'm a monster. I did those things for us."

He stopped and looked at me. "You think it was easy being away from you guys? Missing holidays and birthdays?"

His voice cracked and I forced myself not to go to him. To comfort him.

"I was a kid when I left home. I grew up in strangers'

houses. I missed my parents. I missed you. So don't act like I didn't have to sacrifice anything. I gave up a normal life, a real childhood, to guarantee us a solid future."

I fought back the tears threatening to burst. He was right. I was just as self-centered as he was. I'd only ever seen things from my side. I was the victim. I'd never considered how hard it would have been to live away from home from age twelve. I didn't ever once think about the things he'd given up.

"Erik."

He shook his head. "I can't look at you right now. We'll talk later."

He disappeared down the hall, and when I heard his door shut I fell back on the couch. This was our first real fight. I'd always kept things bottled up. I never let him know how bad things were. I kept a smile for his sake.

On the outside, we looked like the perfect siblings. But really, we were broken. Our family was broken.

This was our chance to make things right. To grieve for all that we had lost and to open up to each other. We'd be stronger. We just needed to get through this.

I stared at the wall and sighed. I hadn't meant to go off on him like I had. I wanted to talk about what he said to Reese, but now Reese was a low priority.

As much as I wanted to sit and wallow, I had work to do. I took my laptop into my room and crawled into bed. I needed to get the pictures from the hospital up on the blog before the weekend. Press would pick up before the game and I wanted to give them as much positive attention as possible.

I was about halfway through when I got to the first picture of Reese. I stared at his smile directed at the little girl lying in bed. She was laughing and looking up at

Reese like he was a superhero. He certainly looked like one.

I clicked through the next thirty images before I got to the end of his pictures. He visited so many children. So many more than he was expected to. Then he went down to the other floor to see those kids.

He was good. He was genuine. He was the kind of man I dreamed of. But I couldn't have him.

I'd been alone so long, I didn't understand why I was stuck on him. I barely knew the man, but my heart knew all it needed to know. There was more to Reese Murray than his hockey statistics. More than his good looks and charm. He challenged me. He didn't expect me to take care of him like every other person in my life. He wanted to take care of me.

Looking at his face wasn't making this any easier.

He didn't date during the season.

I didn't date players.

Erik was against it.

It would be a distraction for the team.

It would only lead to more problems.

So many negatives stacked against us. My head accepted it, but my heart refused.

I needed to take my mind off him. I went to Erik's foundation website and made sure everything was up to date. I loved Schultz Sanctuary. It was a home for women and their children who were escaping a bad relationship and needed a place to get back on their feet. Erik had shocked me when he told me that was what he wanted to do. Most of the guys focus on the youth programs, which was excellent, it just made my brother's decision surprising.

The shelter was a home in Salt Lake he'd purchased, and we hired an entire team with a specialist to help the women. We kept the exact location secret to protect the women, but Erik and I tried to visit a few times a month.

It was something we were both passionate about.

I could tell when Reese told me about his organization how much it meant to him. It blew my mind he helped a thousand kids every year. That was beyond what most people shot for. Of course, he did things bigger than most. He loved kids. I'd witness that at the gala. The most amazing part of his organization was that he didn't name it after himself. He didn't take the credit. There was nothing wrong with either option, but it was another peek into the real Reese Murray.

I opened a new tab and began working on getting him set up. Was I doing this for an excuse to talk to him? Maybe. Probably.

It was also my job to help players with things like this. It was for work.

I could lie to myself all I wanted, but that wasn't going to change the fact that I hadn't gone to these lengths for anyone else.

If I had any sense left, I would treat him like anyone else. I would create space. I would think of him as a brother.

None of that was going to happen.

I shook my head and closed my laptop. I was being pulled in too many directions. My head was going one way, but my heart was digging its heels in. Which one was I going to follow?

Erik made it clear what he thought. Was Reese worth damaging my relationship with my brother?

Maybe.

Probably.

I fell back on my bed and closed my eyes. Things had never been so complicated for me. There'd never been a temptation to go against everything I knew was good for me. This wasn't me.

I was safe. I was routine. I was reliable.

Reese made me want to break out of that mold.

He made me want to be my own person, free of Erik's shadow.

Was I ready for that? Leaving my comfort zone? Going against what people expected me to do?

Maybe.

I sighed.

Probably not.

14

REESE

I could feel her. I didn't allow myself to look into the stands. I couldn't see her. If I had any hope of getting through this practice I needed to clear my mind of her.

I'd been slammed into the glass more times than I could count in the last hour. I was beaten and bruised, but that wasn't what hurt the most. I wanted to go to her. To beg for a shot. It was contrary to everything we'd said, but I couldn't do this. I couldn't pretend I didn't feel something every time I thought of her.

"Get it together, Murray!"

I ignored Coach and skated after the puck. Schultz passed it to me, and I sped toward the goal. I was hit on my left but managed to correct and pass it to Hartman. He scored and turned to me.

"It's about time you pulled your head out of your—"

"Again!" Coach wasn't giving us any slack today. Not that I deserved it.

We ran through plays for three more hours before he finally let us go. I was heading to the locker room when Erik stopped me.

"I want to talk to you."

That was the last thing I wanted to do, but he didn't look like was going to accept a no. He turned and led me to an empty training room.

"What happened today?"

"I don't know, man. Just an off day."

He shook his head. "You're not allowed to have those."

I glared at him. "Excuse me?"

"You're Reese Murray. You're in the top five players in the league. You're a champion. You don't have off days."

I knew my stats—he didn't need to remind me.

"I talked to Sanchez."

"My old captain?"

He nodded. What gave him the right to go behind my back and talk to my old team?

"I wanted to know if this was normal for you. He was shocked. He said you were the only person he's ever known that has been one hundred percent in the game. You've never let outside distractions affect you. So, what's happening now?"

There's never been a woman before. I couldn't exactly tell him that though. He'd kill me.

"There's a lot going on right now. I'm still adjusting to the team."

"Cut the crap. We both know that isn't it." He stepped forward until we were chest to chest. "Figure it out and take care of it. Do whatever you need to do to get your head back in the game."

I narrowed my eyes and studied him. Did he know? Was this him giving me permission to go after Chloe?

I nodded, and he gave me a final look before turning and walking out of the room. I respected him for calling me out, but I was more confused than ever.

While I showered and changed, I thought about what he'd said. If I had any hope of regaining my focus and not screwing up the season, I needed to figure things out with Chloe. Whatever was going to happen, we needed to decide now. Before the season started and mistakes like today affected the whole team.

With my mind made up, I took the elevator up to her office. I walked with feigned confidence and knocked on her door.

She called me in. Would she say that if she knew it was me?

I opened the door and slipped in. I gently closed the door before she had a chance to protest.

She was beautiful. The fight I'd had during practice disappeared when I looked into her chocolatey eyes.

"Chloe."

Her hands hovered over her keyboard as if they were waiting to see if they should keep working or throw a punch at me.

"Reese."

"Are you busy?"

She looked at the screen in front of her then back to me. "No. Do you need help with your foundation? I started some of the paperwork. I just need some information from you."

That would have been a great reason to come talk to her. I wished I had planned ahead instead of storming into her office. "That's not why I'm here."

She cocked her head. "Oh."

"This isn't working."

Her brows pinched together, giving away her worry. "The team? Reese, you haven't given it enough time."

I sat down across from her and fought back a smile. "Not the team."

She leaned forward, her hands folded on her desk. "Then what?"

"This."

Her eyes narrowed, and I smirked. She was adorable when she was frustrated.

"What, Reese? Use your words."

I laughed. "My mom used to say that exact thing to me."

She almost smiled. I could see the corners of her mouth tremble. "Mine too."

I sat back and crossed my ankle over my knee. "I have a problem with the current situation and it's affecting my game."

"I noticed."

Of course, she did.

"I was told I needed to get myself together and fix whatever was on my mind."

"Good. I think you should."

She still wasn't catching on.

"Well, I'm trying."

She looked confused. "Do you need my help?"

"Yes, as a matter of fact, I can't fix it without you."

She sat up straight. "I'll do whatever I can."

That was Chloe. Always putting other people first. Was there a limit to what she would do for someone in need? I hoped so. Thinking of her getting taken advantage of brought on a new sort of anger. One I hadn't experienced before. Was this what it was like to care about someone? The primal urge to protect her was undeniable.

"I just need one thing."

"Anything."

"Go out with me."

"Sure, where?" She reached for her purse, but I held up my hand to stop her.

"Not now."

"When?"

"Friday night."

"Okay."

"Wear something nice." I winked and stood.

"Wait, is it a charity event?"

"No. It's dinner."

"For who?"

"Us."

I could practically see her mind going into overdrive trying to understand.

"Chloe?"

She blinked up at me.

"I'm asking you on a date."

"What?"

"I'll pick you up at seven."

I opened the door and left before she had a chance to turn me down. By the time I got to the elevator I was laughing out loud. Her reaction was priceless. No other woman I knew would ever hear the words "go out with me" and assume it was a favor or for a charity.

Now I had to find the perfect place to take her. Somewhere private. Somewhere the entire team wouldn't be.

15

CHLOE

Getting his address was easy. Getting into his building was easy. Finding the courage to knock on the door? Not so much.

When Reese opened it, he stepped back. Good, I caught him off guard. It was his turn to have someone show up and force themselves into his personal space.

"What are you doing here?" He was smiling but his eyes darted around like he was looking for someone else.

"We need to talk." I held my ground. I almost pushed into his apartment to get out of the hall but figured that would be a bit too much.

"How did you find me?"

"Your address isn't hard to look up." I smiled innocently as his eyes widened.

"On the Internet?" His panic was entertaining.

I almost lied. I wanted to, but that would be cruel.

"I got it from one of the assistants. She had to send out the gala invitations, so she had yours."

He narrowed his eyes.

"Do you want to stay off the grid or something?"

"Nah. I'm just surprised you made the effort. You could have just talked to me tomorrow."

"No. I really couldn't."

"Is something wrong?" He grabbed my shoulders and looked me over.

"No." I felt bad I'd freaked him out. "I just knew I wouldn't be able to sleep tonight if I didn't talk to you."

"You'd be up all night thinking about me?" He winked and I almost left. This. The cockiness. The ego. This was why I didn't date players.

"Ha. You wish." I looked down so he couldn't see my cheeks flush.

"I do."

I ignored that comment. I had to for my own sanity. "I'm worried."

He leaned against the doorframe. He still hadn't invited me in. "About what?"

"About what the guys will think."

His eyebrow raised. "What do you mean?"

"I've been strict about my no dating rule. You aren't the first guy to ask me out from the team."

He seemed surprised. Was it such a shock anyone else would be interested in me?

"I've always turned them down."

"Until me?"

"Yeah. Until you."

"Can't resist me?" He wagged his brows and laughed after a few seconds.

I swatted at him. "Stop."

He cleared his throat and nodded. "Okay sorry. I'm honored you're bending your rule for me."

"I'm not bending it. I'm full on breaking it."

"I know." His smirk grew.

I wanted to wipe it from his face. With kisses. What was wrong with me? This man was messing with my mind. I needed to leave. "I just don't want to give them the wrong idea."

His eyebrows rose. "What would that be?"

Wasn't it obvious? "I don't want them to take it personally that I didn't go out with them."

"Well, it is personal."

"No." Was he always this difficult? If he kept it up my crush, or whatever this was, would quickly disappear.

"Yes. You're going out with me but refused them. That's personal."

I groaned. "I never felt anything with them."

His smirk grew into a full grin. "But you feel something with me?"

Oh boy. This would max out his ego. "Yes."

"Me too."

"So, you'll keep it quiet?" I bit my lip waiting for him to respond, and he took his sweet time considering.

"For now."

That was the best I was going to get. "Thanks."

I turned to leave.

"Do you want to stay?"

"I shouldn't." I really, really shouldn't. Erik would send out a search party if I didn't come home soon.

"Okay."

Okay? Guys were never this calm when I turned them down. I guess accepting a date eased the burn of turning him down for this.

"I'll see you tomorrow."

"Yes, you will."

I got home and hurried to my bedroom. Erik's car wasn't in his spot, so I had time by myself to pick out what I was going to wear tomorrow night and what my excuse would be.

Erik would probably have a date anyway, so I wasn't too worried about him getting suspicious, but I wanted a story ready when he asked me where I was going. Maybe I could tell him I was going out with Kristen. We didn't get together often out of work, but it wasn't rare enough to raise questions. I'd go with that.

I went into my closet and stared at the dresses. He said to wear something nice. How nice was nice though? Cocktail? Black tie? Who knew.

Reese knew.

I didn't have his number. But I could get it. I sent a message to the front office administrator and waited. A minute later I had what I needed.

I called but he didn't answer, so I tried again.

"Hello?" I could hear the hesitation in his voice. He sounded different too. Like he was trying to disguise it.

"Reese?"

"Uhhh..."

"It's Chloe."

I heard him sigh. "First my home and now my phone."

"I know. I should have reversed the order."

He chuckled. "That's not what I meant."

"I know."

"What can I do for you? Or should I let my agent know I have a new stalker?"

I laughed. He didn't.

"If anyone's the stalker it's you."

"Sure."

I laughed and this time he joined in. "How nice is nice?"

"Am I supposed to understand that question?"

"You said to dress nice."

There was a pause. "Okay."

"That can be taken several ways. I need further clarification." I looked over my clothes wishing I could pull the answer from him without the explanation.

I heard him mumble something but chose to ignore it.

"Nice is a pretty dress."

"How formal?"

"You're not going to prom."

I moved away from my gowns. "Okay so like a cocktail dress."

"I don't know what that means."

"Of course not." I closed my eyes and sighed. "Like a dress I'd wear to work or fancier?"

"Whatever you want, Chloe. I don't care."

I wanted to reach through the phone and shake him. "I want to be comfortable wherever we go, and I won't be if I'm over- or underdressed."

More mumbling. I was pretty sure he swore.

"Wear a dress just a bit nicer than what you'd wear to work."

I moved to my date dresses. Okay."

"Did that really help?"

"Kind of. What are you going to wear?" I pushed hangers back so I could look at what I had.

"I haven't thought about it."

Ugh, men. "Think about it now."

"This is already the strangest date I've been on."

"We haven't gone out yet."

"I'm aware."

We were off to a great start. "Just decide."

He sighed. "A suit."

Now we were getting somewhere. "With a tie?"

"No."

"What color?"

"I thought we agreed this isn't prom."

Why was he being so difficult? Hadn't he had a girlfriend before? These were normal questions. "I know, but if you wear a brown suit I don't want to wear a black dress."

"Who wears brown suits?"

"People?"

"In the nineties."

I shrugged. "Men's fashion is not my forte. Erik is way too opinionated for me to even attempt to get involved. So what color?"

"Navy blue."

My mind conjured an image. I was not disappointed. "Good choice."

"Are we done now?"

"Sure."

"Okay. Goodnight, Chloe."

"Goodnight."

I hung up and pulled out a white, lace dress. Hopefully it would work.

16

REESE

Knowing how much thought and energy Chloe was putting into this date was putting pressure on me. I was just planning on going to a restaurant, somewhere fancy, but now I was panicking.

"Hey, Olli." I hurried to our goalie before he left the locker room. Practice was over, and I managed to not completely suck, and I knew the guys would want to get home as soon as possible for our last weekend before the season started.

"What's up, Murray?"

No one else was around so I didn't have to worry about anyone overhearing.

"I've got a date tonight."

His eyebrows shot up. "You move fast."

I ignored the comment and moved on. "I want to take her somewhere special. Not just a restaurant or something."

"You really like her?"

I wasn't about to get gushy with him. "Yeah."

He nodded but didn't say anything.

"You got any ideas?"

"Yeah. I'll make a call."

"To me?"

He chuckled. "Let me put some things in place. I'll give you a call when it's ready."

With that he turned and walked away. I should have stopped him. I should have demanded more answers, but he seemed so confident.

On my drive home, I had to stop myself from checking my phone. Olli was a good guy. He wouldn't flake out on me. I should probably have a backup plan in mind though, just in case.

I parked and waited for my phone to ring.

Maybe a restaurant wouldn't be the worst thing. I could call ahead and ask for a private area.

No. That was lame.

This was a huge deal for me. I didn't date. Especially not the sister of a teammate. Chloe was breaking her rules for me, too. I had to go all out. Make sure she didn't regret this. I wanted her to know how much she meant to me. We'd only known each other a couple of weeks, but I already knew there was something between us. Something worth fighting for.

My phone lit up and vibrated in the cup holder.

"Hello?"

"Be at the Red Butte Gardens at seven-thirty."

"The what?"

"Google it."

"Fine. What's going to be there?"

"A surprise."

That wasn't something I was interested in. "Come on, man. What am I supposed to tell her?"

"It's a surprise." He laughed but I didn't think he was

funny. "Calm down. I have a whole night planned for you guys."

"How did you do that in just a few minutes?"

"You haven't been around very long, so I won't hold it against you that you don't know this. But I'm a pretty big deal."

I laughed. "To some people, maybe."

"Hey! I can just as easily call them back and cancel."

"No." That was the last thing I needed. "I appreciate it."

"Anytime, Murray. Have fun."

"Thanks."

I hung up and hurried up to my apartment. I had an hour to shower and get ready and pick Chloe up.

My suit was pressed and waiting for me in my living room. This was one of the many times I appreciated assistants.

I hurried and got ready and was riding up the elevator with five minutes to spare. It wasn't until I knocked on the door I realized Erik might answer. How was I going to explain this?

My heart was in my throat as the door opened up. Chloe looked gorgeous in a simple white dress. It was perfect, hugging her curves. Her smile dissolved the worries I'd had about tonight.

"Are you ready?" I couldn't stop staring at her. I could spend the whole night right here appreciating the view and go home a very happy man.

"Yeah." She stepped out and locked the door behind her. "Where are we going?"

"It's a surprise." I smiled to myself using the words Olli had said to me while I pressed the button for the elevator.

"A surprise?" I couldn't tell if it was concern in her voice or excitement.

"Don't you trust me?"

"Of course." She didn't hesitate. Either she said it out of instinct or she really did. She had no reason not to, but it was rare for someone to give away their trust so easily.

At my car, I opened her door for her before hurrying to my side. I was more nervous than I was playing my first NHL game. It was just a date. I could do this.

I looked up directions for the gardens on the Internet before coming over. It was closer than I thought it would be. I was glad that Olli had thought of it. I turned down the street and hoped she wouldn't guess where we were going, but she knew the area better than I did. About ten minutes later I caught her looking at me with narrowed eyes, as if she was examining me.

"Are you taking me to the gardens?"

I couldn't deny it, so I just nodded. "Have you been there before?"

"A few times for events, but never just on my own."

"Me neither."

She laughed at my lame joke. "Well, obviously you haven't been before. You've been here for a few weeks, but I doubt this was on the top of your to-do list."

"That's true."

"Then what gave you this idea?"

I didn't say anything at first. I couldn't think of anything fast enough. That was something else I should have planned for.

"It was one of the players, wasn't it?" She paused for a moment. "It was either Porter or Olli. None of the other guys would have thought of a place like this."

I could practically see her mind working. "Do you know everything about everyone on the team?"

"Yes, I do. It's my job."

"Well, then." That made me just a bit nervous. "Hopefully you haven't done this before."

She smiled and reached for my hand. I squeezed her delicate fingers. She didn't pull away, even when we got to the gardens and parked were Olli had instructed me.

"Stay." I held up my hand and she looked at me as if I might be a little insane. She wasn't wrong.

I got out and rushed to her side to open her door. I offered her my hand, and when we got out I laced my fingers through hers and led us to the pathway on the left. Olli said it would be on the far side of the garden.

"How beautiful!" Chloe stopped and admired a section of flowers. The sunset casted a warm glow over the gardens. Chloe turned to look at me and I almost stopped breathing. She looked like an angel with the haze of golden and orange behind her.

"What's your favorite?"

"Lilies." I scanned the area around us, and she laughed. "There aren't any here."

"Oh, well, it's good to know."

She laughed as we continued down the path. She pointed out plants she knew the names of while I just watched her. She was so different out of the arena. It was like a weight had been lifted off her. I wanted to see her like this more often.

We wandered until I spotted the lake. I led us that direction and found the surprise.

There was a gazebo with candles and a single person waiting. Impressive, Olli.

We walked hand-in-hand down the path to the gazebo and the man smiled at us.

"Hello, Mr. Murray and Ms. Schultz. It's my pleasure to have you here tonight. Please take your seats."

Chloe's smile grew when I took out her seat waiting for her. "What have you done, Reese?"

I just smiled and nodded to the man. "What's your name?"

"You can call me James. Tonight, we have a three-course meal. Please relax, get comfortable, and I will bring the salad course."

I nodded and leaned back as he placed two plates in front of each of us. It looked good and Chloe seemed pleased, and that was all that mattered.

"You surprised me, Reese."

"Oh yeah?" If only she knew I was walking into this date blind too.

"I wasn't expecting something so thoughtful."

I felt guilty I hadn't thought of it. "I did have some help." I had to admit it.

She smiled. "I figured." She looked out over the water with a look of contentment.

The sun was setting, casting a warm glow and highlighting her face. She looked like a dream. I wanted to touch her. Graze her cheek. Kiss her lips.

I flexed my hands to distract myself. I couldn't ruin this.

"This is the first date I've been on in..." I had to stop and think. "Maybe two years." Why had I just admitted that?

She turned to face me. "I think it's been about that long for me too."

"What?" I hadn't meant to say that aloud, but I couldn't believe a woman as beautiful and sweet as her could go that long without a guy trying to catch her.

She nodded. "I don't date much."

"Not even outside of the team?"

"No. I don't really meet guys that aren't affiliated with the Fury."

That made sense. Her life was the team. "Is it bad that I'm happy about that?"

She laughed. "If I wasn't okay with my nonexistent dating life I might be offended."

"I'm glad you took a chance on me."

"Me too." She smiled and looked away.

We went through the next two courses with an ease I'd never experienced with a date before. I thought it would be awkward with James around, but he was discreet and gave us our privacy.

When we were done, James stepped forward. "Now, if you'll follow me."

He led us to a garden area already set up with hot cocoa and chocolate covered strawberries. Waiting for us there was a blanket laid out on the ground.

"It's a beautiful night. The sky is clear. You should be able to see quite a few stars."

With a slight bow, he turned and left us alone.

Chloe looked around with a brilliant smile. "This is amazing, Reese. How did you put this all together?"

I would tell her the truth later. Right now, I just wanted to bask in the moment.

We lay down and settled in next to each other, our arms barely brushing.

I tried not to focus on the feeling of her next to me. I needed a distraction. "Let's see if we can spot a shooting star."

She scooted closer to me and rested her head on my shoulder. "That could take a while."

Her vanilla scent was overwhelming. I counted to ten to distract myself from her heat. There was nothing about this moment I would change. "I'm okay with that."

"Me too."

We stayed like that for half an hour watching the sky and pointing out stars, pretending we knew the constellations. I thought I spotted a shooting star once until she pointed out it was a satellite.

I could have stayed there all night, but I heard her yawn. I sat up and looked down at her with a smile. "Let's get you home."

She nodded, and I helped her up before stealing her hand again. I couldn't handle not touching her, even for a moment. Now that my body knew what it was like, there was no surviving without her. If only I knew how she felt. Was this just a date to her, or was it more?

I studied her out of the corner of my eye while we walked back to the car. I caught her glance a me a few times, always with a small smile on her lips.

When we got to her door, she stopped and looked up to me. "This night was perfect, Reese. I couldn't have imagined a better one."

I smiled down at her, looking from her eyes to her lips and back to her eyes.

Was this the moment?

I dipped my head, and when she didn't pull away, I pressed my lips against hers. She pressed against me and let out a small sigh. This was it. This was all I wanted. I could die a happy man now that I knew what it was like to kiss Chloe Schultz.

I definitely owed Olli, big time.

17

CHLOE

I was in so much trouble.

I didn't regret the date, but one night made my life a whole lot harder. I was going to have to lie to Erik, the team, even Kristen.

I didn't know who I was most worried about. They each posed their own threats. Erik would try to lock me in my room forever. The team would call me a hypocrite. Kristen would tease me until I quit. Probably long after that too. She wouldn't let something like this go.

I could only hope that once they all got over the shock they'd be happy for me.

I finally found someone I liked, trusted, and could see a future with.

I changed out of my dress and into my comfiest pajamas. I lay on my bed and stared at the ceiling. What was I going to do?

I couldn't keep this from people for long, but there was more on the line than my inability to keep a secret.

It could throw Erik's game.

I could lose my job.

I shot up. I could lose my job.

There wasn't some written rule forbidding team employees from dating players. That I knew of. But a member of the front office dating a player was definitely frowned upon.

Oh crap.

I had not thought this through.

This was bigger than me. Bigger than my rules. Bigger than Reese and his.

He wouldn't get in trouble. He was a star on the team. It would be my throat on the chopping block.

This wasn't anything I could fix now. For the first time in my career I was dreading Monday.

I sat at my desk pretending to work but really staring at my blank screen. What was I going to do?

I could ask Kristen if she knew of anyone that had dated a player. She had been here longer than me and was always in the know about office gossip. But that would mean telling her. I couldn't just causally ask something like that. I could tell her it was for an article.

She'd laugh.

There was no one else in the office I trusted. It would raise a red flag, and as much as I loathed the idea of giving her something to tease me about, I trusted her. She wouldn't tell anyone.

I sent her an IM and asked her to come in.

I think I can. I think I can.

Less than a minute later she walked in.

"Hey." She sat down and made herself comfortable.

"Hi, could you shut the door?"

She paused and looked at me. Like she was looking into my soul. It was rare for me to have private conversations, but this was confidential.

She leaned back and pushed the door closed. "What's going on? Are you firing me?"

"Oh no! Never!" Guilt filled my belly for even making her think that for a second. "I'm sorry, I didn't mean to make it seem so ominous."

"Sure. What's going on?" She was as on edge now as I was.

"Have you ever heard of someone up here dating a player?" I blurted it out before I could chicken out.

She held up a finger. "Wait, what?"

She heard me. I knew she did. She just wanted me to say it again. I narrowed my eyes and waited.

"What's this about?"

"An article."

She laughed out loud. "No, it's not."

"Just answer the question." My blood pressure was reaching unnatural highs.

She leaned back and folded her hands on her lap. "Yes."

"What happened?"

"What do you think happened? The guy had one bad game and management blamed her. Guess who got fired."

Crap. This was exactly what I feared.

"Really?"

She smirked. "No. I just wanted to prove we weren't talking about an article."

"You're evil."

"And you're a rebel. What happened to swearing off players?"

I shrugged.

She leaned forward with a Cheshire cat smile. "Reese Murray happened?"

I nodded.

"I knew it. So, give me the dirt."

"Not until you tell me the truth. Has anyone dated a player?"

"Not that I can think of, but you're fine. You're a part of the team. Plus, think of what Erik would do if they fired you."

"He'd probably stage a walk out." The idea made me sick. I wouldn't allow the team to get involved.

"They won't fire you as long as your boy performs."

"Erik though."

She shuddered. "What did he say?"

I didn't answer, and her jaw dropped. "I know before Erik? This is the best day of my life!" She clapped. "Oh. Can I be there when you tell him?"

I narrowed my eyes. "It's not funny."

"You might want a witness there. Just in case."

"It's not like he'll hurt me."

She frowned. "I think you overestimate his self-control, Chloe. You're his sister. His twin. He's been protecting you since you were little."

I wanted to correct her. Tell her about the fight I had with him. He wasn't the super brother everyone thought he was. We'd grown up separately. We'd only been inseparable since college. Since our parents…

"I'm sure he'll be cool about it."

I raised an eyebrow and she laughed.

"Okay. He's going to lose his mind."

"That's why I can't tell him. Not when the season is about to start. I don't want this on his mind."

"Sure, and there might not even be anything to tell."

"What does that mean?"

She smiled at me like you would a child. "Chloe, you haven't dated very much, so you still have high expectations. Guys tend to have short attention spans, especially players."

Was she saying Reese would get over me? Soon?

"It's nothing personal, and maybe Reese is different." She cringed, just enough for me to notice. "You may not have to even tell Erik because this whole thing could be over soon."

Well, maybe she was right. Maybe Reese would move on in a few days. That was the reputation of most of the guys. They dated around, never staying with one girl for long. Plus, Reese was new here. Why would he want to tie himself down to me?

"You're right." I tried to smile, but knew I was failing. "I won't worry about telling him yet."

She leaned forward and grabbed my hand. "Chloe, I wasn't trying to be cruel. I swear, I just don't want you to get hurt."

I squeezed her hand. "I know. I appreciate it."

She pulled away and stood. "Let me know if I can help at all."

I nodded as she left, shutting the door behind her.

Our date had felt real. Our chemistry was real. Was this just a fling for him?

My heart begged me to go down to the ice and find him. Ask him for his side. But that was the first step. I would distract him during practice. Then it would be during a game. He'd start making mistakes and he'd blame me. Then the team would blame me.

Wait. How had I gone from a single date to destroying the team's season?

Kristen was right. I was getting ahead of myself.

I just needed to take things one day at a time. Friday had been perfect. I hadn't heard from him since, but that wasn't strange. Erik had been gone all weekend too. Practices had picked up in preparation for the first game. He was busy.

Too busy to text me?

No. Stop. I couldn't start thinking like that. I wasn't going to sabotage this before it really even started.

I'd talk to him tonight.

My phone vibrated on my desk. It was a message from Emma wondering where I was. I was missing a practice. My absence had been noticed. It would probably raise more questions if I missed it than if I stayed hidden away in my office.

I was first and foremost Erik's sister. He told me over and over again how important it was to him that I was there to support him.

I could do this without giving anything away.

I closed my laptop and left my office. It was a normal day. Normal practice. I would work and watch my brother just like I did every day.

When I got to the seats the Pride had taken over they all clapped.

"We were missing you!" Sasha called from the other side of the row.

I waved and took the empty seat next to Emma. "How are they looking?"

"You can feel the nerves. Only two days until the game."

She was right. There was an energy in the arena that hadn't been there last week.

"They'll be fine."

She nodded. "He's looking good though."

I looked up but didn't see Erik on the ice. "Where?"

She pointed across to where Reese was talking to her husband at the goal.

"Olli always looks good. That's why we keep him."

She laughed and bumped her shoulder against mine. "You know that's not who I'm talking about."

I looked at her and she winked. She knew? How did she know?

"Olli told me about the date."

I narrowed my eyes. "What date?"

She laughed harder before taking a breath. "Oh, honey. Calm down. I'm not going to tell anyone."

So, it was Olli that planned it. I knew it wasn't Reese on his own. "Well, now I know who to thank. It was a perfect night."

"I'm glad. It's about time."

"For what?" I looked down at my laptop, but I wasn't going to get any work done. I hadn't seen the girls in three days and I knew there would be gossip to catch up on. Plus, I wanted to pump Emma for all of the information she had.

"You."

"Me what?"

"You've been here for, what, four years?"

I nodded.

"And you've been working with the team for two of those?"

She knew this, but I didn't know what she was trying to point out.

"Yes, Emma."

"And I've known you for that entire time."

"Yes?"

"I've never heard you talk about a guy, never heard of you going on a date, never seen you look at one of the guys."

"They're like my brothers."

"But not Reese."

"I guess not."

"I'm just excited that someone finally caught your eye. He's a good one, too."

"I think so."

"How did Erik take it?"

I kept my mouth shut, and she started laughing. "Oh, honey! You are in so much trouble."

I was so glad she and Kristen were so entertained. "How about you tell him?"

"No way!"

I cringed. "Olli?"

"He likes his face the way it is."

I closed my eyes. "Hartman?"

"I don't think that's a captain's responsibility."

I sighed and leaned into her. "What if I get the whole team to stand between me and Erik when I tell him?"

She patted my arm. "That might be necessary, but not for you. For Reese."

"Oh yeah. I should probably wait until the season's over so they don't kill each other."

She wrapped her arm around my shoulder. "Give both of them a little credit. They're professionals. I'm sure they can keep their personal feelings off the ice."

I doubted it.

"You'll have to tell him soon. He'll want it to come from you. Don't let him hear it from someone else."

That would be much worse for everyone involved. But I hoped I could get away with it for a little while longer. One date wasn't anything to get upset over. Maybe if things got more serious. Then I'd tell Erik. Yeah, it could wait.

When I got back to my office, Kristen was blocking the

door holding a letter. "This came for you. Is Erik starting another charity?"

I took the envelope and read the address. The Utah Department of Commerce. That was fast.

"No, it's for Reese's."

Her eyebrow raised. "Oh yeah? Then why are you getting mail for it?"

"Because I'm helping him."

I turned and walked into my office, but she followed. "Are you helping him as the Marketing Director or as Chloe, the beautiful single woman?"

She was smirking, but I ignored her. She was like a child bully. The only way to beat her was to not give her the attention she wanted and hoped she went away.

"Single woman it is."

"Out."

She left my office laughing and closed the door. If I didn't love her so much I'd request a new assistant.

I pulled out my phone and sent Reese a text that we were ready for the next step. I told him I was available tomorrow to work on it if he wanted.

I finished the rest of my work while checking my phone every few minutes. He never replied. Had I broken a rule? Was I not supposed to text him so soon after our date?

I slumped in my chair. This was why I didn't date. It was too stressful. I hated constantly doubting myself.

18

REESE

I'd been able to avoid Olli for a few days, but he finally cornered me after practice to talk about the date like we were teenage girls. I told him it had been a nice night, but he wasn't satisfied. I wasn't allowed to leave until I told him we'd kissed. He hit me on the back with a wide smile.

"Atta boy."

"You've been married for too long."

He looked up to the stands to where I was sure his wife, Emma, was sitting and shook his head. "It's never long enough."

I mock gagged and left the ice. So far none of the other guys knew about my night with Chloe, which was perfect. It also meant I could trust Olli.

I hurried to shower and change. I wanted to talk to Chloe before she left. I hadn't called her over the weekend because I didn't want to pressure her. I didn't want to come on too strong, but I'd been second-guessing that decision since I saw her walk down the stairs in the area. She looked beautiful, but she never met my eyes. I could sense from yards away there was something between us and I wanted to clear it before it turned into a major obstacle.

I waved bye to the team and hurried down the hall toward the elevator. I pressed the button when someone said my name. I turned and saw her standing halfway down another hall.

"Hey." I hurried to her before anyone came out of the locker room and saw me talking to her.

I pulled her into my arms the moment she was within reach. She smelled like vanilla and I inhaled her. "I missed you."

She laughed against my chest. "It's been two days."

"I'm sorry."

She pulled back and looked up at me. "For what?"

"Not responding. I got busy after practice yesterday."

Her fingers rubbed over my sore back muscles. "Don't worry about it. Just don't do it again."

"So, I get another chance?"

She bit her lip and I nearly bent down to kiss it.

"This time."

I finally let her go, but instantly missed her warmth.

"What are you doing down here?"

"I wanted to see you."

That had to be a good sign. "And risk Erik seeing you?"

She peeked around me. "Yeah, although we should probably find somewhere safer."

I took her hand and led her out to my car. I opened her door before looking at her. "Have dinner with me?"

She nodded and got in.

When I started the car and drove out of the parking structure, she seemed to relax.

"Where are we going?"

"My place?" I probably should have checked to see if she

was comfortable with that before assuming. I watched her reaction out of the corner of my eye, but she just nodded.

"Are you going to cook for me?"

Wooing a woman with my cooking was not one of my moves. I had maybe three meals I'd mastered, thanks to my mother, but I doubted she'd be impressed by spaghetti with canned sauce.

"I'm going to try."

She giggled, making me smile. "This is a first for me."

That simple statement made my ego swell. I was the first guy to cook for her. Probably the first guy to take her to dinner in a garden.

Too bad I was also the first player she's dated.

The first one she's broken her rules over.

Did that mean my strikes evened out?

We were walking through the door when she stopped without warning. I stumbled into her, grabbing her shoulders to keep her from falling over. "What's wrong?"

"It's so bare."

I looked around at the blank walls, single sectional sofa, and TV. "It's functional."

"It's sad."

I pushed her inside and shut the door behind me. "It's not like I've had a ton of time to add any personal touches to the place. I've been at the arena more than I've been here."

She nodded while looking around. She made herself comfortable, showing herself to the kitchen. "At least it's modern."

It was that. My agent found two options to choose from while I was on the flight here. I'd picked the one closer to the arena. Not much thought over the paint color or appliances had been put in.

"It doesn't seem like you're planning on staying long."

She eyed the suitcases that lined the hallway back to my bedroom.

"I haven't had time to unpack. My assistant offered, but I feel weird about someone else dealing with my laundry."

She smirked. "Then what does your assistant do?"

"He keeps track of my schedule, grocery shops, manages my fan mail, and answers my email."

She nodded slowly. "That would be nice."

"Doesn't Erik have one?"

She laughed. "You're looking at her."

I had to take a second to calm down. "That's not your job."

"Not technically, no. But I do keep track of his schedule, grocery shop, and manage his fan mail. He answers his own email, though."

I was sick of talking about Erik and him taking advantage of her. That seemed to be one topic we couldn't agree on.

I moved around her to the fridge and found it stocked with plenty of options. "How does ravioli sound?"

She ducked under my arm and peeked in. "You can make that?"

I pulled out a bag of premade ravioli. "I sure can."

"You're a cheater."

"I'm resourceful." My assistant was good at not only grocery shopping, but meal planning. He wrote out a week's worth of meals at a time and left recipes for each. I picked up the ravioli's and looked it over. A brown butter sauce. That didn't sound too hard.

We worked around each other as I made the sauce and she prepared a salad. I wasn't used to having people in my space. Even in Boston, I rarely had people over. I thought it would feel weird, but it didn't. We seemed to flow together.

She didn't stop to ask where things were. She'd check until she found it, and by the time dinner was ready she knew my kitchen better than I did.

I set the dining room table for two and brought the plated food out. "Madame." I pulled out her chair and waited for her to sit.

"This is so nice."

It was the best I had to work with. I wished I had candles or some nice wine to offer, but I didn't drink during the season. I'd have to add candles to the shopping list, though.

I held up my water glass and she mimicked me. "To many more nights like this."

She smiled and clinked her glass against mine. "Cheers."

"I should have learned after the first date not to underestimate you."

I looked down at the pasta. It wasn't that fancy.

"I'm not talking about the food, although this is really good."

"Then what is it?"

"It's just you. I keep thinking you'll drop the act and end up being just like all the other players. Crude, selfish..."

"That makes us sound horrible."

She shrugged. "I guess I just expected the worst. Maybe that's why I never wanted to date any of them before."

"And none of them are me."

She smiled. "You're right."

"So, what is it about me?"

"Are you, Reese Murray, digging for compliments?"

I laughed and lifted my arm to rest on the neighboring chair. "I'm just interested."

"It was probably the offensive things you said when we first met."

I cringed. I hadn't understood the dynamics between her

and Erik. I still didn't, but I hadn't had the mind to shut up. "I'm sorry about that."

"I'm not." She looked at me, not smiling for the first time that night. "You made me realize I wasn't living my own life. Sometime over the last few years, Erik's had taken over. I might not have liked that you pointed it out in front of the team, but you were right. It was time for me to stop living in his shadow and leave my comfort zone."

"I'm glad you took a risk on me."

"Me too."

We ate the rest of dinner with much lighter conversation and cleaned up in comfortable silence.

"Would you like to stay? We can watch a movie."

She smiled up at me. "I'd love to some other time. We both have early mornings. I should get home."

"Of course."

We drove back to the arena and I pulled up next to her car. She reached for the door handle, but I stopped her.

"Let me." I got out and went to her door. I wanted to prolong our goodbye, but she was right. We both needed to act like responsible adults, no matter how badly I wanted to stay up with her all night. I felt like we'd only skimmed the surface and I wanted to dive deeper. To know all of her. Her past, her fears, her hopes.

"Thank you for tonight." She looked up at me through her lashes and I nearly caved. I didn't want her to go.

"Thank you for coming." I wrapped her in my arms and breathed her in one more time. When I stepped back, she stood up on her tiptoes and gently kissed my lips.

"Goodnight." She whispered against my cheek before slipping away and getting into her car.

19

CHLOE

The guys had promotional events all week. From meeting the mayor, pictures with fans, and now a parade. I was covering them all for the blog and site. It was still warm outside, but a crowd had formed along the street to see the players drift by on themed floats. This was one of the last chances for the public to see the team before the season started. The players threw candy to the children, and at the end of the route, people could get autographs and pictures with their favorite players.

It was a fun tradition, even though I was sweating through my team T-shirt.

Things were going perfectly. Kristen was monitoring the floats and promised she'd deal with any problems that arose, but I was still waiting for something to go wrong. With so many pieces involved, it was bound to happen.

I'd been talking to reporters this morning, so I wasn't able to talk to the guys. I wanted to wish them luck and remind them to hang out at the end to interact with the fans. Hopefully, Kristen or one of the other assistants told them.

Taking pictures was a good excuse to be around because

it was the only time I would be able to see Reese, or Erik. Everyone was so busy. They had interviews and photoshoots almost every day, plus practices had been grueling. It was exciting, and as much as I loved the start of a new season, it was always hard to adjust to it. Life felt like it moved in fast forward.

"Hey, Chloe! Take a picture of us!" Porter and Hartman were sitting on the top of a vegetable garden-themed float waving to the crowd with wide smiles. I held up my phone and got the shot. I gave them a thumbs up and kept walking down the road to the next float.

Our photographer, George, was taking pictures of the guys, so I wasn't worried about missing anything, but these would be good shots for the guys to post on their social media accounts later. Fans loved this kind of stuff.

I took pictures of the crowd and each float to get a feel of the atmosphere so I could write about it later. I let the floats pass me, waving to the players and snapping pictures.

"Hey, Chloe!" Erik was standing on top of a beach themed float surrounded by beautiful women in bikinis. It stuck out with all of the family-friendly floats in the parade, and I wasn't surprised Erik had found it.

What did surprise me was who was standing on the back. With two model-thin scantily clad women hanging over him.

"Hi, Erik." I took a picture of him for future blackmail and waited for the float to pass.

Reese noticed me when it was far too late for him to cover up what was happening.

His smile disappeared in an instant. I could see the panic on his face, and his lips formed a curse, but it was too late.

I looked away and walked down the road.

What was he thinking?

He was a player. On and off the ice.

I should have seen it coming. He was a star. Soon he'd be a full-blown celebrity here in Salt Lake. It was bound to go to his head sooner or later. I should have known.

How stupid could I be?

He could have any woman in the world. Why on Earth had I thought he'd be interested in me?

Stupid. Stupid. Stupid.

I shook my head and pasted on a smile for the crowd. I couldn't let it get to me right now. I had work to do.

As each float passed, I cheered with the crowd. The last float was carrying Coach Romney and Coach Rust, who were met with applause. They were heroes in the city. They'd led the team to the playoffs for the past seven years with two championships. People loved them just as much, or maybe more, than the players.

They waved to the crowd and I followed behind the float. A few members of the front office were walking the parade route, so I joined them.

Kristen slipped her arm around my shoulders. "Hey! I found you."

"You're supposed to be watching remotely. What if something goes wrong?"

She laughed. "You need to relax, Chloe. I put Greg in charge. I wanted to be at the fan event in case you needed me."

I cringed. I didn't want to go and see Reese there. The bikini girls would probably be all over him.

"Can you actually run that?"

She dropped her arm looked at me with shock. "Are you serious?"

I nodded.

"You're delegating?"

"Don't act so surprised."

"What an honor. Chloe Schultz is passing responsibility onto my meek shoulders." She held her hand up to her chest. "What have I done to deserve this extortionary honor?"

"Don't make me regret it."

She smiled and patted my arm. "I got this."

"Thanks. I'm going to head back."

I turned and headed in the direction of the arena without giving her any more details. I didn't want her asking why I didn't want to be there. It was petty. It was immature. But it was avoidable, so I was going to take advantage of it. I had enough to write an article. I didn't want to wait until the end to see Reese wrapped up with even more girls.

I walked back to the arena and hid in my office. Since everyone else was down at the parade like they were supposed to be, I knew I wouldn't be bothered. I opened my computer and wrote up a quick article and saved it so I could upload it once I had pictures. I sent out the ones on my phone to the guys so they could post them later.

There was more I could have worked on at the office, but I was mentally done. The more I thought about Reese the more frustrated I got. Sitting in my office stewing wasn't accomplishing anything, so I gave in and went home.

This wasn't anything a bath and pint of ice cream couldn't fix.

By the time I settled into the warm water my mind was in overdrive.

Were those women what Reese wanted?

Rail-thin with a big chest?

Fake tan and blonde?

The complete opposite of me?

It was stupid. I shouldn't compare myself to them. They were models. They were probably nice girls, too. Dang it. That made it a lot harder to hate them.

Not that they were the problem.

It was me.

It was Reese.

He was a superstar.

I was a nobody. The sister of somebody.

I blinked back the tears that were threatening to explode and leaned my head back against the porcelain.

20

REESE

I didn't need to talk to Chloe to know she was mad. Even Erik noticed, which was an accomplishment considering he was surrounded by models and enjoying himself far more than I was.

I'd wanted to jump off the float the moment I saw her, but that wasn't really an option. I was there for work. I was representing the team. I couldn't let my personal feelings distract me from my job. Was it my job to be on that specific float? No. Could I have found one without bikinis? Probably. Okay, yes.

But Erik had approached me and asked to pair up. We were supposed to have a few guys on each float, so I agreed. I didn't know he'd already called dibs on the sunscreen float. He was in heaven and enjoying every minute while I was in my own personal hell. The girls were nice, but I wasn't attracted to them in the slightest. Not that I could convey that to Chloe when she saw me.

I should have known better than to go anywhere with Erik. He was trouble.

No, he wasn't.

He was a single guy. He probably thought he was doing me a favor. As another single guy.

I couldn't say anything. I couldn't tell him I had a girlfriend. Was Chloe even that? We'd been out twice. Three times if you count the tour, which she didn't.

If I'd said no to Erik, he would have asked questions. Questions I wasn't ready to answer. Chloe was adamant about not telling him and I wasn't going to take that choice from her, but there were consequences to that decision. Like having the guys on the team assume I was a single man who would enjoy the company of some single women.

As soon as I was able, I ran back to the arena to talk to her.

The front office was empty. Her office was dark.

By the time I got back to my car, I knew she'd likely gone home. Not just because she lived there, but because she'd think I wouldn't show up. She thought Erik was enough of a deterrent.

She was wrong.

I cared more about her than about Erik rearranging my face.

I rode up their elevator thinking of an excuse to be there. If Erik opened the door, I'd have to say something. Give some explanation for being at his doorstep.

I needed to borrow something? What? I had everything he did when it came to gear. We didn't have any formal events, so it's not like I needed a tie or suit. A book? Ha! Like Erik was a reader. Maybe I'd just say Chloe asked me to come over. For an interview.

Yeah.

I knocked feeling more confident.

Erik opened the door and just a bit of that confidence disappeared.

"Hey." He eyed me.

"Hey, I—"

"Who is it, Erik?" Chloe's voice was like a sucker punch to my gut. She didn't sound like herself. She sounded sad.

"Reese."

She came around a corner and stopped. Her red eyes seared my heart. I'd done that. I was the one that caused her sadness. I wanted to run. I didn't deserve to be near her.

"What do you want?" Erik pulled my attention away from the girl who had changed my life.

"I got a message that Chloe wanted to ask me some questions." His eyes narrowed. "For the blog."

He looked over his shoulder. "Did you want to talk to him?"

She sniffed and looked to me. "Not really. But I have to."

Erik stepped back and waved me through.

"I've got to go in a few minutes, but if you need me let me know." He was looking at his sister and I had a feeling they were somehow communicating without words.

"Okay."

He disappeared down the hall, and I took a second to look around. Anything to avoid her dejected eyes.

I understood why Chloe was so shocked by my place. Their apartment felt like a home. Warm paintings, pillows, photographs, and decorations filled the space. It wasn't overly feminine either. It was comfortable, lived in. I wanted to take a closer look at the family in the pictures, but now wasn't the time.

I turned and walked to her. I wanted to take her in my arms. I wanted to kiss away the tears. I wanted to take back today.

"I'm sorry."

She looked down at her feet, which were covered in fuzzy white slippers. "For what?"

I almost laughed in frustration. She was going to make me work for this. Good. I deserved to be punished.

"I'm sorry that I allowed myself to be in that position. I'm sorry I let any woman who isn't you within five feet of me. I'm sorry that I put the opinions of other people before yours."

She looked up at me with watery eyes.

"Why?"

"Erik asked me to partner with him." I shrugged. "I thought it was a good idea."

"He never has good ideas."

I held back a laugh. She was making jokes. That was a good sign.

"I realize that now."

"You looked pretty happy up there."

"Those young women were funny."

She glared.

"I didn't want to be up there with them, Chloe. I would have rather been with you, but since that wasn't an option I should have switched floats, but I didn't know how without raising questions."

She nodded. "That would have been strange."

"Yeah. I couldn't think of a logical reason that wouldn't come down to me not wanting to be around those women."

"I get it."

"You do?" I should have been relieved, but she was still hurting.

"Yeah. I realized something, too."

"What?"

"That you belong up there with those beautiful women.

You're a star. You're gorgeous. You're young. You should be out there dating models and partying with Erik."

I put my hands on her shoulders and waited for her to look at me. "Chloe, please listen to me. I'm not your brother. Other than being hockey players, we have nothing in common."

She smirked, but it only lasted for a second.

"I don't want to be partying. I don't want to date models. I just want you."

I stopped before more words spilled out of my mouth. Words neither of us were ready for.

"Why would you want me? I'm a nobody."

I shook my head. "You are my somebody. You're smart, witty, breathtakingly beautiful, and you care about everyone around you. To a fault."

She smiled again, and I dipped my head until we were eye level. "I chose you, Chloe."

Another tear fell from her eye. I leaned forward and kissed it away. "No more tears."

"Those were the happy kind." She said in a small voice.

"No more." I pressed my lips against hers. This is how things were supposed to be. Her in my arms. Us together.

"I'm leaving," Erik called out.

I jumped away from her at the sound of his footsteps coming closer.

"Bye," Chloe called out with a red face.

"See ya tomorrow."

He didn't bother looking back as he waved and opened the door.

When it shut, Chloe sighed and leaned against me. "That was close."

"Good thing he lives in his own world."

She tugged on my shirt until she had my attention. "Thank you for coming."

"Always." I hugged her before stepping back. "I'm also here to ask a favor. I know I'm not really in a position to do so, but..."

"What is it?"

"I know we've only been out a few times and we haven't known each other for very long..." I trailed off not knowing how to ask.

"Reese, what is it?"

"The game's tomorrow."

She nodded. Obviously, she knew.

"My parents are coming to see it."

Her smile took over. "Can I meet them?"

"That was what I was going to ask."

"Of course! I'd love to meet them."

Wow. That had been a hundred times easier than I thought. I didn't know how the subject of parents would go over. I didn't want to make her sad or uncomfortable. We'd talked about her parents and their deaths, but I wasn't sure how she felt now.

"Thank you."

"I'm excited. When do they get in?"

"In the morning, so I was hoping we'd meet them for lunch. They'll be in a box with some of the other parents for the game. You can join them."

She shook her head. "The pride sits down low."

I knew that, but I didn't want her to think she wasn't invited. "Right, of course."

"I'm so excited."

"There's one more thing."

Her eyebrows shot up. "What else?"

"I was wondering how I can introduce you."

"What do you mean?"

I looked around as if an easy answer would suddenly appear. "Do I introduce you as my friend? Coworker? Girlfriend?"

I mumbled the last word, but judging by her surprised expression, she'd heard.

"Oh, Reese." She bit her lip while I prayed for the floor to open up and swallow me whole. I was suddenly in middle school again.

"As long as they can keep a secret, I'd like them to know me as your girlfriend."

Had I heard her right? I looked at her smile. Her eyes. She was serious.

"Really?"

She nodded.

"Thank you." I kissed her quickly. "Okay, I'm leaving before anything else can happen to change your mind." I began walking backward toward the door.

"I'm not going to." She was laughing and following me.

I reached behind me for the doorknob and opened it. "I'll see you tomorrow."

"Okay." She put a hand on my chest and reached up to kiss my cheek.

My body felt like it was going to explode. I couldn't remember the last time I'd been this happy. "Bye."

"Bye, Reese." I'd remember that smile forever.

21

CHLOE

I held Reese's hand in the lobby of the Grand America Hotel. My palms were sweating, and I wanted to wipe them off, but that would mean releasing my vice grip. This was my first time meeting the parents. I'd never had a serious enough boyfriend to warrant this. What if they didn't like me? Would Reese dump me? He was such a gentleman, I couldn't imagine his parents being awful, but what if they were? Could I stand to be around them for the rest of my life?

Okay, I was getting ahead of myself. We were dating, not engaged.

I smoothed my peach, pleated dress with my free hand and reminded myself to breathe. This wasn't going to be scary. They were going to be lovely.

"Calm down, Chloe," Reese whispered and kissed my temple.

"I'm nervous." I stared ahead, waiting for the elevator doors to open and reveal Mr. and Mrs. Murray.

"They're going to love you."

Reese was their only child. If I had to guess, he was close

to his parents. His mom would likely see me as a threat and hate me. His dad would think I wasn't good enough for his only son. I wasn't worthy to carry on the family name.

"Stop thinking."

I let out a sigh. He knew me so well already.

A ding sounded, and I looked up at the doors. A middle-aged couple stepped forward and smiled when they saw Reese. His mother was a beautiful woman. She was about the same height as me and wore cream slacks with a light pink blouse. Her bobbed, dark hair was the same color as Reese's. His father was an imposing man, just like his son. That's where Reese got his height from. His salt and pepper hair gave him a distinguished look with his navy suit.

"Honey!" His mom hurried forward, and Reese dropped my hand to meet her. They hugged, and I could tell by the way she squeezed him how much she missed him.

He stepped back and gave a hug-backslap to his dad.

"It's good to see you, Reese."

"I'm glad you guys are here." He moved back next to me and grabbed my hand. "I'd like you guys to meet my girlfriend, Chloe Schultz."

I watched his mother's expression for any sign of anger, but she surprised me by extending her arms and wrapping me in a hug. "Reese has told us so much about you, Chloe. I'm excited to finally meet you."

"You too." She released me and stepped back, still holding my hands. "You are even more beautiful than he said."

I could feel my cheeks warm at her compliment. I wasn't used to a mother's praise.

"Thank you." She released my hands and wrapped her arm around Reese.

"Don't embarrass her, honey." His dad looked to me. "It's a pleasure, Chloe."

I smiled at his dad. "Thank you, sir."

"Call me Carl." He winked, and I felt myself relax. "And my wife, Karen."

Karen beamed at me and nodded. They didn't hate me. They were warmer and more inviting than I could have dreamed.

"Let's eat." Reese led us to the garden where he'd made reservations for lunch.

After we sat down and ordered, the questions began.

"Tell us all about yourself, Chloe."

I smiled but panicked on the inside. "What would you guys like to know?"

Carl smiled. "Start with your family. Where are you from?"

"We're from just outside Calgary."

"Oh, that's such a beautiful area." Karen hadn't stopped smiling since she laid eyes on Reese, and it was rubbing off on me.

"It is."

"Do you go back there often?" Carl broke off a piece of bread and handed it to his wife before taking a piece for himself.

"Not since high school."

I could see the question in his eyes, so I continued before making him ask. "My parents passed away just before graduation."

Karen gasped. Her smile was gone. I hated that I'd cause that.

"It's okay." I smiled even though I hated that part of death. The consolation I had to offer people when they found out my parents passed.

"I'm sorry, Chloe. I just can't imagine how hard that would be to lose your parents so young. And to be a mother and not be able to see your child grow up." She covered her mouth with her napkin.

"I appreciate it. My brother and I had each other, though."

"You have a brother? Oh, that's lovely." She smiled, but it still held sadness.

"A twin, actually. We became close after losing them. As you could image."

Carl nodded. "And what does he do?"

I looked to Reese who shrugged. "I guess he hasn't told you?"

His parents looked confused. "My brother is Erik Schultz, the Fury's right wing."

Carl shook his head. "Of course. I should have connected your names sooner."

"Your brother's a player?"

I nodded. In more ways than one, Karen.

She eyed Reese. "That was a risky move."

"She works for the team, too." Reese challenged.

Carl smirked. "Of course, she does."

"Oh, Reese." Karen suddenly looked disappointed.

I knew this was too good to be true.

"Mom, we're both adults. It's not a big deal."

"What does your coach think of that?"

I cringed. He was the least of my worries.

"No one knows."

That had Carl laughing. "Oh boy."

I leaned forward before Karen could panic anymore. "It's my fault. I haven't wanted to tell my brother."

Karen looked at me with a frown. "Why not?"

"He's pretty overprotective." Reese coughed, and I shot

him a look out of the corner of my eye. "I didn't want to cause any stress for the team with the season about to start."

Karen pursed her lips.

His dad looked between us. "So, you're keeping it a secret."

I hated the way his dad made it sound. "For now, yes."

"That's a good idea."

I had to close my mouth to keep from gaping. He agreed?

"Your relationship is new. There's no point in causing drama if it doesn't work out."

I started nodding until I realized what he was inferring. He didn't think we'd work.

Reese finally spoke up. "Dad, it's not like that."

"Would you like to tell the team?"

Reese inhaled sharply. He met my eyes for a second before nodding. "Yeah, I would."

Carl nodded like he understood everything. He didn't. How could he?

"It's a complicated situation." How could I get them to understand?

"We understand, Chloe." Karen's smile had returned, but it was dim. She didn't like the situation either.

I suddenly felt like a complete idiot. They probably thought I was using their son. What woman in her right mind wouldn't want to claim him?

"I'm going to talk to my brother."

"Oh?" Karen looked from me to Reese.

He was looking at me though. "You are?"

I nodded. "Soon."

He smiled and grabbed my hand under the table.

"Well, then. Let's move on to the real problem at hand." I

looked from Reese to his dad. "The Miami Sharks have a tight defensive line. What's your strategy?"

I sat back and let them discuss the game while forcing myself to eat. I hoped I hadn't ruined things with his parents. I didn't understand why they were so interested in whether or not our relationship was public. How did it affect them?

Then I thought of my parents. They would be concerned if the guy I was dating wasn't willing to tell his family about me.

They would be disappointed in me now. They didn't raise me to run and hide from confrontation. They encouraged me to go after what I wanted. To not take no for an answer. When it came down to it, Erik didn't get a say in my relationships. I wanted him to approve. I wanted him to support us, but if it meant I moved out and put some space between us for me and Reese to be together, I would do it.

I didn't like being pressured into things, though. And right now, I felt like I would only be doing it to please Reese's parents.

I would do it on my own time. Soon, but not today.

There was a lull in the conversation, so I jumped in. "Reese told me about how beautiful Michigan is, especially in the summer."

Karen smiled. "It is. I just wish he was able to come home more often."

Reese shook his head. "I get out there as often as I can, Mom."

"Oh, I know. I just wish we were closer."

"You're always welcome to move here."

Carl balked. "I'm not selling our home to jump around the country with you."

"I've only moved twice in my career."

"He's right, Carl. Maybe we should think about moving." She winked at me when Carl wasn't looking.

I watched the interaction, amused. Karen was joking, but it was stressing out Carl.

"Not a chance! Ann Arbor is our home."

Reese was the first one to crack. "We're kidding, Dad. I would never expect you to move. I'll just have to try to get home more often."

That seemed to placate his parents, but I knew he wouldn't live up to it. The season was unrelenting. He might have one or two days off around the holidays, but his life wasn't in his control. I was sure his parents knew that too. It can't be easy being so far from your only child, though.

After our dishes were cleared, I reached into my bag and pulled out two boxes. "Reese told me you guys didn't have these yet, so I wanted to make sure you were game ready."

I handed them their boxes and watched. They looked at each other, then opened them.

"Oh, Chloe! Thank you." Karen held up the jersey and showed it to her husband.

"That's very kind, Chloe." Carl patted the jersey looking down at the name across the back.

He looked up and focused on Reese. "I'm proud of you."

"Thanks, Dad."

We stood and exchanged hugs. We returned to the hotel lobby and Reese took my hand again.

"I'll see you guys after the game."

His parents nodded and headed back to the elevator.

22

REESE

The energy in the locker room had me buzzing. Everyone was pumped for the game. We'd been waiting for this night, and the time had finally come. After the lunch we had, I'd been excited. It went better than I could have expected. My parents texted me telling me how much they loved Chloe and how great we seemed together. It was the first time that they'd really approved of my girl-friend. Normally they could find flaws until the intrigue vanished. I thought they'd fixate on the fact we were keeping it a secret, but they didn't seem too worried after Chloe said she would be telling Erik soon.

It was the first time I'd ever pictured a future with some-one, and knowing my parents liked her made it all too real.

What if this was it? What if she was the one?

I wanted to be rational. We'd only known each other for a few weeks. It couldn't possibly be serious yet. Could it?

"Murray! You ready?" I looked up and nodded to the captain. Hartman looked as calm as ever. He wasn't the type to let the excitement get to him.

Erik, Hartman, and I stood together at the entrance to the tunnel, waiting for them to announce the starting line.

Hartman turned to face us. "Fury! Are you ready to win?"

Erik and the guys behind us made a roaring sound I'd learned was our battle cry. I joined on the second one and Hartman held up his stick before running out to the ice. I followed behind Erik, but nearly stopped when my first skate hit the ice.

It was the first time I'd been in this arena with the crowd cheering for me. The sound was near deafening.

It was exactly what I needed for this game.

I warmed up with the team, trying to keep my attention on the ice, but I wanted to find her. I wanted to know where she was and if she was watching.

It wasn't the right time, though. I was here for one purpose. To win.

My thoughts had to be in the moment, not twenty feet up the stands.

The national anthem and coin toss passed in a blur. It was time. I took my position behind Hartman in the faceoff.

We won the puck drop and the game started. Erik took possession of the puck. I pushed through their line up to the left of the goal and turned. Hartman had the puck, and, in a flash, it was sailing toward me.

I passed it to Erik, who was open. He hit the puck at an impossible angle and it flew past the goalie's head and into the net.

The crowd exploded. Erik and I bumped fists and the rest of the line crowded around us.

"Keep this up!" Hartman was smiling, and I knew I'd taken a major step in his eyes. I was officially part of the team.

The rest of the game seemed to go in fast forward. I played over twenty-eight minutes, and I was still full of energy when the buzzer sounded for the end of the game. I joined the team in the center and received a few slaps and pats on my back. It had been a great game. I had one point and two assists, and we'd won six to one. Olli kept shaking his head, and Hartman told me he was hoping for a shutout on the home opener, but one goal was nothing to be upset about.

We'd performed as a team. All issues and distractions had been left in the locker room. One game and I felt like I'd been with these guys forever. They were my home now.

I skated to where Olli was waving. "Where are they at?"

He looked at me and grinned. "You didn't look?"

"No. I wanted to stay focused."

"Sure." He pointed a few rows above our bench. Emma, his wife, and Chloe were in a group of women wearing black and red shirts.

Chloe saw me looking at her and smiled. I waved, and she gave me a thumbs up.

"Come on, we need to stretch and get changed out before we miss the party."

I followed him in, high-fiving Hartman as I walked past the bench.

Coach was standing in the middle of the locker room clapping. "Great game, Fury! I liked the teamwork. I liked the effort. Let's keep this up."

He left, and I hurried to shower and change. I had a feeling there would be press waiting to speak to some of us. I'd managed to avoid them on the way into the locker room, but they would always be waiting after.

Olli was sliding on his shoes when I walked over to him while slipping on my suit jacket. "Ready?"

"Yeah, man." I grabbed my bag and headed down the hall with him. No cameras were waiting for us, so we were able to go straight to the fourth-floor banquet room.

We walked in and cheers erupted. Some of the guys were already there, so the group must applaud anytime players walk in. Olli waved and patted me on the shoulder. "They're over here."

I followed him to a table in the back where Emma was sitting with Chloe and my parents. They stood up when they saw us, and Emma hurried to kiss Olli. "You did so good, babe!"

I turned away from their love fest and greeted my parents.

My dad clapped me on the back with a wide grin. "That was a great game, Reese."

"Thanks, Dad."

Mom wiggled between us and kissed my cheek. "You were amazing, sweetie! I haven't seen you so relaxed in years."

"This is a great team. I'm lucky to be here."

"They're lucky to have you." She hugged me before finally letting me near Chloe.

I wrapped my arms around her and breathed her in.

"You really were amazing, Reese. You and Erik seemed to read each other's minds." She looked up at me with a bright smile.

I looked down, taking in her deep, honest eyes and perfect lips. "It's weird how natural it came."

"This is going to be a good season. I can feel it."

"Me too, baby." I kissed her forehead before realizing we were surrounded by players, team employees, and plenty of cameras.

I stepped back and looked around. "Where is your brother?"

"He hasn't come in yet."

There had been a few people still in the locker room, so it made sense. I still wanted to be careful, though.

"I'm starving."

"Take a seat. I'll have the waiters come around." She turned and disappeared into the crowd.

I sat down at the table with my parents and Olli and Emma joined us. Chloe returned and sat next to me. Within a minute, food appeared and I dug in without a second thought.

I was only halfway done when the rest of the guys walked in, followed by the coaches. Erik looked around and waved to Chloe but stayed at the front of the room.

"Do you normally sit with him?" I realized I was probably impeding on their traditions.

"Not really. I'm normally mingling, and he looks for someone to take home." She said it with a bit of venom. I knew he had the reputation of a player, but this was the first time she acknowledged it.

The rest of the players and their families took seats, and Coach stood up in front of the room. It quieted quickly while we waited for him to speak.

"That was a great start to what I know is going to be a terrific season. I'm proud of the work of everyone here." He looked around the room. "Players, will you please stand?"

I looked around to see the other guys following his direction.

Coach began clapping and the audience soon followed.

"Now, guys stay standing. If you're someone that supports a player. If you're family, an assistant, agent, work in the front office, or you just love the Fury, please stand."

Everyone else stood and Chloe placed her hand on my back. It felt so good having someone with me for the first time. My parents were always supportive, but having her by my side was different.

"Take a look around. We are all here for the same reason. We love this team, we love these players, and we want to win!"

The audience applauded again, and someone popped a bottle of champagne. Immediately, several more bottles followed. That only encouraged the crowd, and soon music was playing.

I turned to Chloe and placed my hand on her cheek, feeling her warm skin with my thumb. I dipped my head, kissing her with the adrenaline left from the game.

Whooping around us finally brought me back to the present.

The eyes of everyone at our table were on us. Emma was beaming, but Olli was looking at me like I'd lost my mind. I turned slowly to see Erik charging at us. I stepped in front of Chloe, blocking her from his wrath.

I lifted up my hand and stepped forward. "Great game, Schultz."

He paused, first eyeing my hand, then my face. "What's going on, Murray?"

I dropped my hand and shrugged. "Just celebrating the win."

"By kissing my sister?"

I looked back at Chloe and turned back to him. "I just grabbed the closest woman."

He looked at me, his eyes narrow and his fist clenched. "Chloe?"

She stepped beside me looking nervous. "Hey."

"You let him just kiss you?"

She blinked rapidly. "It just happened. We were celebrating."

Erik looked back to me. "She's not just some woman you can grab and kiss, Murray. Disrespect her again and we're going to have a problem." He looked back to his sister. "Come sit with me, Chloe."

I waited for her to object. To tell him she was staying with me, but she walked past with without a glance at me.

Once they walked away, our audience went back to their own dinners. I sat down to see my parents looking at me with clear disappointment.

"Oh, Reese." Mom was shaking her head, and Dad reached for her hand.

Emma was glaring at me, and Olli offered me a single shrug.

What had I done wrong?

Sure, I got caught up in the moment. I kissed her in front of the team. I knew that broke our unspoken rule, but I played it off.

I doubted she wanted me to take that opportunity to announce to the entire room we were dating.

We'd work it out later. I was sure she understood.

23

CHLOE

Erik seemed to relax once we were at his table. He didn't bring up the kiss again and went back to talking with the guys. I smiled at the right times and nodded like I was paying attention, but I wanted to disappear.

He'd blown me off so casually. He just grabbed the nearest woman to kiss? He was covering up our relationship, but did he have to make it seem like I was just some bimbo off the street?

He could have said it was a friendly kiss or that Erik misunderstood. He just brushed me off like I was nothing. In front of his parents. In front of our friends.

It was humiliating.

Did he really feel that way?

Of course not.

Right?

This night was going to last forever. Dinner wasn't even over yet. Then there would be another speech from Coach, and probably Hartman. Maybe some drinking and dancing. At least two more hours.

I couldn't do it. I wasn't going to last without exploding. Or breaking into tears.

"I'm not feeling so well." I leaned over to Erik and patted his arm.

He looked me over. "Are you okay?"

I shook my head. "I'm going to head home."

He stood and helped me out of my chair. "Are you okay to drive?"

"Yeah, I'll be fine."

"Okay. Call me if you need me."

I gave him a quick hug and hurried out of the room. Part of me expected Reese to follow, but as soon as I was in the elevator, I knew he wasn't coming.

Each inch of distance I put between us felt like I was headed toward the end.

It all had been too good to be true.

By the time I got home and changed into my comfiest pajamas, I'd convinced myself it had never been real. He was just having fun. Getting a taste for his new city. He'd been using me.

I grabbed a pint of ice cream out of the freezer. It was hidden behind the frozen fruit where Erik would never think to look. He didn't eat sugar or dairy during the season and wouldn't let it in the house. I had a stash of treats hidden in strategic places where I knew he wouldn't find them. Right now, nothing was more important than my mint chocolate ice cream and my bed. I didn't care if Erik walked in and saw me with the forbidden fruit...cream.

I turned on a comedy, something dumb with no romance whatsoever, and crawled into bed.

Despite my efforts to shut off my brain, I couldn't. I replayed the last few weeks, wondering where I'd let myself fall.

I wouldn't be hurting this bad if I hadn't.

We went from having fun to something more, but when? How did I not notice?

At least I didn't have anything to remind me of him. No photos of us. Not even a single sweatshirt.

Just a shared workplace.

I wouldn't be able to hide from him forever, but they wouldn't have practice tomorrow, so I had at least one day to pull myself back together.

It would probably take longer than that.

The movie was almost over when Erik appeared in the doorway. "How are you feeling?"

I'd had the sense to throw away the evidence of my pity party, so I just nodded. "I'm doing okay. Thanks for asking."

He stepped further into the room and sat at the end of my bed. "The guys missed you. They didn't have anyone to laugh at on the dance floor."

"Hey. I'm a good dancer." I tossed a pillow at him, but he caught it.

"I'm kidding. You were missed though." He leaned back on his elbow and watched me.

"Thanks. I'm sorry I left."

I was sorry. It was the first team event I'd missed. Well, I was there for the beginning, but...it wasn't like me. I couldn't let someone change my life. I wasn't going to run from him. I wasn't going to miss out on anything else. This wasn't just Reese's team. It was Erik's. It was mine.

"Next time." He stood up and walked to the door but stopped before walking out. "Is there anything I can get you?"

"No, I appreciate the offer though."

He nodded but didn't leave. "Are you sure you're okay?"

"Yeah." I needed him to go. The longer he looked at me like he was waiting for me to crack the sooner I would.

"Okay, good night."

"Night." He shut the door and I fell back into my bed. I wasn't going to be able to lie to him for long. We knew each other too well. He wouldn't let me blow him off again. I'd have to talk if I didn't pull myself together.

I could do that. I could be strong.

Tomorrow.

I chose a new movie and cuddled in with my pillow. It was about halfway through when my phone vibrated on my nightstand. I ignored it. Erik was home, Kristen wouldn't be calling this late, and neither would any of the girls from the Pride. That left one likely option, and I wasn't interested in speaking to him.

As soon as the vibrating stopped, it started again.

This went on for over five minutes. I reached for my phone to turn it off when it started again.

Reese Murray.

Seeing his name hurt.

He'd thrown me away.

I silenced it and stared at the screen.

What could he possibly have to say? He was sorry? He didn't mean it?

Even if he believed that, I didn't want to hear it. There were a million things he could have told Erik in the moment. He'd chosen the wrong one.

A text came in. *If you don't answer I'm coming over.*

That wasn't a threat I was willing to challenge. I couldn't hold Erik back if he found out Reese had hurt me. Or that we were together.

I probably would let the fight happen.

No. That would be a disaster. The last thing I needed was to drag this out or get Erik involved.

I waited for him to call again and answered.

"What?"

He paused. He probably hadn't expected me to answer. "I'm sorry, Chloe."

His voice clawed at my heart. I would not give in. I would not cry again.

"I'm sure you are."

"What was I supposed to do? What did you want me to say?"

His voice was so dejected. Maybe he was as upset as I was. Doubtful. I wasn't sure what the best course of action would have been, but making me seem like some random chick like he did was the wrong thing.

"Chloe, I'm so sorry. I never meant to hurt you. That's the last thing I want."

I sighed but didn't know what to say.

I wanted to forgive him. I wanted to forget the whole night.

He was respecting my wishes. I wasn't ready for people to know about us, and he did what he could to keep it that way.

"Reese." What was the point of hurting us both? "I know you did what you thought was right in the moment, but it hurt."

I heard him sigh. "Chloe, I swear if I could redo tonight I would. I never meant to—"

"I know." I cut him off. He didn't need to apologize anymore. I could hear in his voice how much he cared. "Honestly, I don't know that I would have done anything better."

Every scenario I could think of involved pretending to be

drunk, admitting we were together, claiming amnesia, even denying the kiss happened. None of them would have worked. None of them were perfect solutions.

It's a crappy situation.

One that I put us in.

The realization stung. If anyone should be apologizing, it should be me.

I'd been an idiot tonight. Way too sensitive. Too irrational. I let my emotions run away with my sanity.

"I'm sorry."

"Me too, Reese."

"Can I see you?" I wanted to run out and throw myself into his arms, but we both needed time to feel normal again.

"Tomorrow?"

"Okay."

I hung up and fell back into my pillows.

I wanted him. I wanted to be with him. I just needed to trust him. He was worth it. I wasn't going to let the fear take over. Tonight could have been my excuse. I could have used this as my reason to bail, but when it came down to it, I wasn't willing to give up. I still wasn't ready to tell Erik and the team about us, but I wanted us to work.

24

REESE

Chloe opened the door wearing a black dress and a smile. "Hi."

I cleared my throat. "Wow. You look amazing."

Her hair was pulled up, exposing her neck and shoulders.

"Thanks." She stepped out and closed the door behind her.

We moved to the elevator and I had to force myself to look away. I couldn't get enough of her. Especially after last night. I thought I was about to lose her. She could have ignored my calls. She could have told me she was done. She didn't.

"Chloe, about last night—"

She wrapped her arms around my neck and looked up at me. I could drown in the chocolate pools of her eyes and die a very happy man.

"Don't. Please. Let's just forget it happened."

"Of course." I kissed her gently before the elevator bell dinged.

She forgave me, and I was so grateful. I couldn't imagine being on the team, seeing her every day and knowing I couldn't have her.

Once we were in my car I turned to her. "I hope it's okay that I made us reservations at the Golden Palace."

She's told me that was her favorite Thai restaurant when she'd given me the tour. She didn't answer right away. I looked at her and she was staring at her purse.

"We can go somewhere else if you want."

She shook her head and reached into the bag and pulling out an envelope. "I was just hoping you'd go to see *The Founders* with me."

I'd completely forgotten about the show. I hadn't paid a lot of attention to the date on the tickets. I figured she'd already gone and took Erik or a friend.

"Are you sure you want me to go with you?"

She finally smiled. "Of course."

I started my car and headed to the theater. "We only have twenty minutes. Are you going to be okay without dinner?"

"Yeah, we can go after."

I reached over and took her hand. I felt bad for forgetting about the show, but I was honored she wanted to share this with me.

I pulled in front of the theater and let the valet take my car. Chloe was standing on the sidewalk looking shocked.

"What's wrong?"

"You let someone else drive your car?" I couldn't tell if she was appalled or surprised.

"Yeah? That's what the valet is for." She still didn't look like she understood. "It's just a car." A fairly expensive Porche, but still just a car.

"Erik would never..." She trailed off then turned to me. "You're not Erik."

I shook my head. "Thank heaven for that." I wrapped my arm around her shoulder and we walked into the theater.

It was a modern building, and much larger than any of the theaters in New York. The lobby was so grand, I felt out of place wearing jeans and a button-down. If I'd known we were coming here, I would have put forth more effort. Gotten us a limo. Arranged a nice dinner before.

I should have paid better attention to those tickets.

Although, at the time I never would have thought she'd ask me to go with her. How far we'd come.

An usher led us to our seats, just two rows back from the stage. Chloe's jaw dropped, and she turned to me. "This is amazing!"

It really was. I was going to have to give Bryce a raise.

We settled into our seats and Chloe opened the playbill and excitedly pointed out different actors and told me about them.

This was better than I expected. She was like a child meeting her favorite princess. When the lights dimmed, she squeezed my hand and smiled at me. She looked so happy. I wanted to lean over and kiss her, but the music started and I didn't want to take away a second of the show.

I tried to watch the performance, but Chloe's reactions were too charming. She laughed, cried, and sighed throughout the first half. Seeing her face light up was all I ever wanted. Making her happy was my new mission in life. If I could freeze this moment for her I would. I'd do anything to see her like this every single day.

During the intermission, we walked through the lobby to stretch our legs.

"Is it everything you have ever hoped and dreamed of?" I

meant it as a joke, but Chloe was nodding so fast I thought her head would fall off.

"Reese, this is amazing. I don't know how I'll ever repay you."

I could think of a few ways, but I had a feeling she wanted to see the second act.

"You don't have to. I'm just glad to be here with you."

"Thank you." She stood up and kissed me before pulling back and looking around.

Right.

We were in public and heaven forbid someone see us together.

"Let's get back." I took her hand and reminded myself to respect her wishes. She wanted time. That was all. I could wait for her.

When the actors took their bows, Chloe stood and clapped. If she could have jumped on stage and hugged each of them I knew she would have.

Once people began leaving, I took her hand. "That was pretty good."

She looked up at me with glittering eyes. "Good? That was perfection! Thank you, Reese." She stood up on her toes and kissed me quickly on the lips. Before I could react, she stepped back and smiled.

I guess the high of seeing the show lessened her inhibitions.

"If that's all I need to do for a kiss, I'll buy tickets for every night."

She laughed and led me down the row and to the exit. "If only that were possible." She sighed. "This has been one of the best nights of my life."

Well, that's all a man ever wanted to hear. "I'm glad." I

handed my ticket to the valet and pulled her against me. "Thanks for sharing it with me."

I bent down and kissed her soft lips. This. This was all I wanted. Everything with Chloe felt right. Her lips, her touch.

She sighed and pressed into me as I cupped her neck.

Someone coughed behind me, but I ignored it.

"Mr. Murray?"

I groaned and stepped back from Chloe. She had stars in her eyes when she blinked up at me. I smiled and turned, keeping my arms around her.

"Yes?"

The teenage valet boy was standing next to my car with the passenger door open. "Your car is ready, sir."

"Right."

Chloe laughed and broke free of my arms. She slid into the seat while I tipped the kid. I would gladly get anything she wanted to get that reaction from her. Puppy? Diamonds? A car? No problem.

"Um, sir?"

I looked at the valet trying to focus on the present. "Yeah?"

"Would you please sign this?" He handed me a trading card he'd pulled out of his wallet. It was my rookie card.

I almost laughed. "Of course. Do you have a pen?"

He nodded and reached into his pocket.

I took it from him and signed my name.

"Thanks, Mr. Murray. I'm a huge fan. When the Fury announced you were on the team, I lost it. I mean I really did. My mom came into my room cause I was screaming so loud. She didn't get it, though. She's not a hockey fan. But I am. I can't believe I'm meeting you. I drove your car. Wow. I drove Reese Murray's car. This is the best night of my life."

I waited for him to calm down before handing the card and pen back to him. I'd made two people's nights. Huh. Not too shabby.

"Thanks…"

"Oh. Ryan. I'm Ryan Fina."

"Thanks, Ryan. I hope you can make it to a game."

He nodded. "Oh. I will, Mr. Murray."

"Alright, you have a good night." I turned and walked to the driver side.

"I will."

I waved and got in. Chloe was grinning like a mad woman. "You have a fan."

I nodded and pulled away from the theater. "I guess I do."

"Feels good, doesn't it?"

It had been a surprise. I didn't think people here would recognize me. "It does."

"Enjoy your anonymity while you can. Your time is running out before people start recognizing you and mob you everywhere you go."

I laughed. "Does that happen to Erik?"

She shrugged. "Sometimes."

"Well, I am a better player than him."

"So humble, too." She smirked.

"The fans are going to love me."

"They will." She laughed. "How about dinner now, Hot Shot?"

"Oh, you're hungry?" Her stomach had growled during the last part of the show. I felt bad again that I hadn't planned better.

"Starving."

"And you expect me to feed you?" I teased. Her eyes narrowed even though she was still smiling.

"Listen here, Mr. Murray." Her attempt at being threatening was humorous. "You've got to feed me or I'll get hangry. You don't want that to happen."

"Oh no. I wouldn't want that."

"I didn't think so." She sat back and directed me to a burger joint.

Only Chloe could leave a night at the theater and be okay with fast food after. Any other woman would have wanted a fancy dinner, but not her. Just another thing I loved about her.

We sat in the car eating our burgers and watching people in the restaurant.

"I know how to show a lady a good time, am I right?"

She wiped the corner of her mouth and smiled. "You are. This is perfect."

I grabbed a fry from the bag. "I'm sorry I didn't get us reservations for somewhere nicer."

"You think anything else would sound better than a greasy burger and fries right now?"

I watched her lick her lips and smile.

"No, I don't think so. This is pretty perfect."

She nodded. "I think so too."

I reached for her shake, but she swatted my hand. "I warned you to order your own. I don't share."

I pulled my hand back. "I was just checking."

She looked down at the cup and sighed. "You did buy it. If you want some you can take a sip. But only one."

I wanted to kiss her. She was perfection sitting next to me eating fast food in my car. She was a no-frills woman. She was everything, and somehow, she'd chosen me.

"I appreciate your willingness to sacrifice, but I don't like vanilla shakes."

She smiled. "Neither did anyone in my family. I learned to like them so no one would steal it."

I burst out laughing. "That's genius!"

She nodded. "I know." She took another bite and smiled at me.

"You're amazing."

25

CHLOE

I needed to do something to show Reese how much he meant to me. He'd upped his game, so I wanted to make sure he knew I felt the same. I'd made some calls and used a few favors people owed me to set up a surprise.

Everything was ready. The right people had been contacted and the word had been spread. Tomorrow was the big day, and the last thing to do was get Reese there.

"Hello?" He sounded a little out of breath.

"Hey, how are you?"

"Good. Just at the gym with Olli and Hartman."

"Oh no. Are they killing you?"

He scoffed. "I can hold my own with those two."

"I'm sure you can." There was nothing for me to be nervous about, yet I was dreading asking the next question.

"What are you doing?"

"I'm still working, but I was wondering if you're free tomorrow?"

Someone dropped weights in the background. "Sorry. I'm free."

"Great. I'll pick you up at ten."

"Okay. See you then."

I hung up and spun my chair around. "Kristen!"

She came rushing into my office looking around. "What's wrong?"

I put my feet down to stop spinning. "Everything is ready."

"For?"

I rolled my eyes. "You know what."

She laughed. "It's all I've been working on for the past few weeks. I'm well aware everything is ready."

"Are you going to be there?"

She nodded. "I wouldn't miss it."

I closed my computer and stood. "Let's head out then."

She held up her hand. "Excuse me? You're leaving early?"

"Yeah?"

"You never leave early." She narrowed her eyes. "Am I missing something?"

"Nope. I just thought you'd like to get home early since you're kind of working tomorrow."

"Huh." She turned and left the office. I followed her and laughed as she grabbed her purse and led the way to the elevator. She wasn't wasting any time.

When we got to the parking garage, she waved and headed for her car.

"I'll see you tomorrow," I called after her, but she got in her car without responding.

Fine. Now I needed to keep myself busy for the night so I didn't blab to Reese.

I knocked on Reese's door exactly at ten. I'd been standing in the hall, waiting, but didn't want to seem too eager. The last thing I wanted was for Reese to guess what was happening.

"Hey."

I smiled up at him. He was wearing a plain, black T-shirt and jeans. Good. I wasn't going to have to make him change.

"You ready?"

"Yeah. Are you going to tell me where we're going?"

I pressed the elevator button and turned to him. "Absolutely not."

He nodded. "Interesting. Neither would any of the guys. I'm beginning to think you're all conspiring against me."

Good thing I had thought to tell the team to keep their lips sealed.

"You're going to have fun, I promise." When we got down to my car, he opened my door for me before getting in. "You're such a gentleman."

He laughed. "It feels strange not driving."

"Just sit back and relax."

"I'll try."

I met his eyes and smiled. He made me so happy, I just hoped today showed him how much he meant to me.

"It's about a forty-minute drive, so get comfortable."

I pulled out and headed toward the freeway. It was a good thing Reese was new to the area. He wouldn't be able to guess where I was going.

He grew more alert once I pulled off the freeway and headed to our final destination. I tried not to laugh as he read signs and asked me if that's where we were going. He had no idea.

Even as I pulled into the parking lot and stopped, he was looking around, completely clueless.

"Where are we?"

I got out and ignored his question. "Come on and see."

He took my hand as we walked into the building.

"Surprise!" The crowd of reporters, team members, the mayor, and some parents yelled, causing Reese to step back.

"What?" He squeezed my hand. "What's going on? It's not my birthday."

I smiled up at him. "Welcome to the first day of Murray's Youth Hockey for Utah."

His jaw dropped and he looked around. Erik, Olli, and Hartman were standing at the front of the group with a few other members of the team.

Kristen stepped forward with the official plaque we had made to commemorate the date. "Congratulations, Reese."

I positioned him for photos the press requested for the next few minutes before taking him to the ice.

"This arena was used for the Olympic hockey games when they were held here. Now it's home to your foundation, and there are some people here who want to thank you."

I stepped back and gave a signal to the kids skating. There were only about a hundred of them, but this would be our first phase of the year. I was determined to help Reese meet his goal of one thousand kids a year. We would do it, slowly.

The kids cheered and held up a banner that said, "Thank you, Reese Murray."

I watched his expression change from confusion to pure happiness. He rubbed his hand over his jaw as his smile grew.

"You did all this without me knowing?"

I shrugged. "You did the paperwork. I just put things into motion." I nodded over my shoulder. "This is the first group of kids. All of their gear has been provided for free, and we have a team in place to teach lessons. They're pretty excited to meet you, though."

He nodded. "I don't know what to say."

"Then shut up and get your skates on." Erik shoved Reese's skates at him before stepping onto the ice. Olli and Hartman followed.

"Thank you, Chloe. I can't tell you what this means to me."

He stepped toward me and I had to fight the urge to kiss him. I hugged him instead. Once we separated, I pointed at the skates. "You should probably get out there."

He nodded and laced up his skates. The moment he stepped out, a crowd of kids formed around him.

He was laughing and smiling for the next hour as he skated with them. Erik and Hartman had them form lines to take shots at Olli, who was nice enough to bring his gear. They gave the kids pointers and took time with those that were struggling.

A few of the other guys had set up cones and were having kids run drills with them. Reese bounced between groups, cheering people on and helping a few get comfortable on skates.

"My cold heart is melting." Kristen appeared next to me and leaned against the boards.

"It's pretty cute isn't it?"

Watching Reese working with kids was my new favorite thing. I could watch it for days and not get sick of it.

"We did good."

I nodded. "We did. Thanks so much for your help."

I owed her big time. Like a new car or something. If only

I had the money to do something that grand. I could dream about it though; she deserved it.

"Do you think it's time to tell everyone?"

The good feeling I'd had all day vanished. Gone. Goodbye, bliss.

I took a deep breath to keep from saying the first thing that came to mind.

"Not yet."

"The longer you wait the more it's going to hurt."

I shook my head. "Things are going well right now. I don't want to ruin that."

"Hey." I turned to her and waited. "I know you. Keeping something this major from Erik is killing you."

I couldn't deny that. This was the first secret I'd had since we moved in together. His reaction was the only thing keeping me from telling him right now. I didn't want him to be mad. I didn't want something to come between us. We were in a good place, and I wasn't willing to ruin that.

Did that mean I was willing to sacrifice things with Reese?

"Why do I have to have one or the other?"

She watched me for a moment. "Who says you do?"

I wasn't surprised she understood my question. Working closely together for so long allowed us to get each other's meanings even when we were doing poor jobs of communicating them.

"Erik is going to freak."

"What if he doesn't?"

I couldn't fathom that. There's no way he would be okay with me dating one of his teammates.

"I don't think you're giving your brother enough credit."

Too bad I knew him better than she did.

"I'll talk to him eventually."

She shook her head. "Fine."

I expected her to walk away, but she stayed and silently watched the kids with me.

After the kids left and we cleaned up, Reese and I headed home.

"Chloe, I really don't know what to say. Today was one of the best days of my life."

I smiled at him and squeezed his hand. "That's all I wanted. I knew how important this was to you and wanted to make sure it happened fast."

"You're incredible." He lifted my hand and kissed it.

26

REESE

I was itching to see her. To have her in my arms. After everything she'd done for me with the foundation, I wanted to show her how much it meant to me.

I needed one night to show her how much she changed my life. One night to prove what we had was real.

I woke up with an idea. I just hoped she loved it. I sent her a message to be ready at five and put my plan into action.

She told me her favorite flowers while we were at the gardens, so I ordered those to have waiting for us. I hoped if I included a few little touches from our time together she'd realize how much I cared.

I was a mess standing at her door. I needed to knock. I knew that, but part of me wanted to put it off until I calmed myself down. I'd never been like this before. I'd never been so excited to see a girl. It was like I was experiencing my first crush all over again, times one hundred. I'd never felt this way about a woman, and I wanted to show her...without sweating.

The door opened, revealing a smiling Chloe. "What are you doing?"

I took her in. Her long brown hair was flowing over her shoulders like melted chocolate. She looked so beautiful in a black dress that showcased her long legs.

"I was going to knock."

"The elevator dinged a while ago."

She'd heard it. Great. I shrugged and she laughed while grabbing her purse off a table.

"Where are we going?"

Before I could respond, she guessed. "It's a surprise, isn't it?"

I took her hand and pulled her into the elevator. "Of course, it is."

It felt so much better being with her. My nerves disappeared the moment I had her hand in mine.

In the garage, I opened her door for her before getting in. We were heading to her favorite restaurant. She hadn't taken me to it, but on the tour she gave me she mentioned it in passing. I had to beg the owners to stay open for dinner since they normally only had lunch hours, but it would be worth it when she realized where we were going.

A vibrating sound disrupted my thoughts.

Chloe reached into her bag and pulled out her phone. "Oh no."

"What's wrong?" Her expression made me think it wasn't someone she wanted to talk to.

"It's Erik."

Yup, that would make me scowl too.

"Hello?" Her voice didn't give her away. She sounded happy to talk to him.

"Yeah, I was there." Silence. "I'm going out to dinner

with a friend." She sighed. "Because they drove...just some of the girls."

I knew she wasn't going to tell him, but it still felt like a punch to the gut that she lied about me. I'd agreed to keep things quiet, but for how long?

When she hung up she looked at me with a frown. "I don't know how long I can keep lying to him, Reese."

"Then let's tell him."

"What?" Panic filled her voice. "Reese, there's too much at stake."

"He's going to find out eventually." Wasn't he? How long could she keep us a secret? Unless she didn't think we were going anywhere.

"I know, but..." She faded off leaving me to fill in the blank with worst case scenarios. If she wasn't willing to tell her brother, the person she was closest to, then why were we even doing this?

"Chloe. I can't live like this anymore. Look what happened after the first game."

She sighed and tossed her phone into her bag.

"I'm not ready yet."

"So, you got mad at me for trying to cover it up in front of the team, but you're doing the same thing right now." I needed to calm down.

"I told you, I'm sorry. I shouldn't have gotten so upset about that."

"Well, now I understand why you did. How long are we going to lie to the people around us? You're an adult, Chloe. Your brother can't control you. The team won't care. The front office won't care. So, what's stopping you?"

She was silent for a few minutes. Then she whispered something, but I couldn't hear.

"What?"

"I'm scared."

That surprised me.

"Scared of what?"

"That they'll hate me."

I hadn't expected that. "Who?"

"The team."

I looked over at her, but she was staring straight ahead. "Chloe, you care way too much about what everyone thinks. They love you, and frankly, I don't think they'll care who you're dating."

She turned away from me and looked out the passenger window.

I'd upset her, but it was true. She needed to get over her fear of what other people thought of her and decide if being together was worth it.

I pulled the car into the turning lane and made a U-turn.

"Where are we going?"

I ignored the question. I couldn't answer her without this turning into a fight. I drove back to her building and parked but didn't make a move.

"I don't think I can do this anymore, Chloe." She turned to me, and I fought to ignore the tears in her eyes.

"What are you saying?"

"I can't do this secret dating thing. It's not fair to either of us. I know it's stressing you out and I hate not being able to hug or kiss you anywhere I want."

Desperation filled her eyes. "I told you. I'll tell them when I'm ready."

I rubbed my hand over my face. "I know. But I'm ready to tell people and I don't know if you'll ever be."

Her chin trembled. "Don't do this, Reese."

A tear fell down her cheek and I nearly broke. "I'm sorry. It's just not healthy."

I reached toward her to wipe away her tears, but she pulled back.

"I care about you, Chloe. I want to be together, but I can't do it this way."

"Fine." She pushed open the door and hurried away.

This was a hundred times worse than opening night. This time I'd hurt her intentionally, but hearing her lie to Erik was my breaking point. We weren't doing anything wrong, and I was sick of sneaking around like we were.

27

CHLOE

This was the worst. I'd felt pain before. My appendix had ruptured in high school. I thought that would be the worst I'd ever experience.

This was worse.

Reese leaving me was a shock. It had torn me in two.

I thought our first fight was bad. If only I'd known what was going to happen. I wouldn't have answered his call. Why bother apologizing if it wasn't going to be any different?

He expected me to suddenly be okay with going public?

He knew I wasn't ready. That didn't change.

So why had he?

I pushed open the front door and went to my room. I took off my dress and changed into sweats.

There better be ice cream. I had a feeling there wasn't, but I needed something to hope for.

I went to the freezer and pulled the drawer open.

My stash was gone.

No.

Not okay.

My heart was pounding against my chest. How could this happen?

I should have paid better attention last night.

How could I let this happen?

I blinked back the tears, but they were stubborn.

I sniffed.

I was not leaving my house.

Good thing I lived with one of the biggest celebrities in the city.

I picked up the phone and called down to the lobby.

"Yes, Ms. Schultz?"

"Can someone run to the store for me?"

"Of course. What would you like?"

"A pint of mint chocolate chip ice cream."

"Is that all?"

No. I wanted Reese.

"Make it two."

"It will be sent up right away."

"Thanks."

I hung up and moved to the living room. My favorite blanket was waiting for me, folded on top of an armchair.

It was a blanket I'd made with my mom when I was little. We were supposed to learn to quilt together, but we ended up sewing the pieces together and sending it out to be finished. We promised not to tell anyone we cheated.

I wrapped it around me and fell onto the couch.

I shouldn't have let him leave. I should have fought for him.

The line had been drawn. He was ready for more—I wasn't.

The black screen of the TV was a mirror. Disgusted with myself, I turned it on and chose an action movie. I didn't want to watch myself fall apart.

A moment later, I heard the elevator ding. I waited for the doorbell, but heard keys going into the lock.

Crap.

Erik was supposed to be gone all night.

He walked in, took one look at me, and frowned.

"What happened?"

I shook my head. My throat was swollen closed.

He crossed the room and sat next to me. "Chloe, tell me what happened. Are you hurt?"

I nodded and fell apart. He pulled me into his arms and I soaked his white shirt with my tears.

He rubbed my back, asking me again and again what happened, but I couldn't speak.

The doorbell rang, so he slipped away from me and answered.

"For Ms. Schultz."

"Thank you."

I heard the door shut and Erik returned. "Two pints? Must be really bad if you already burned through your stash."

I looked up at him, shocked. "You knew?"

"Who do you think keeps it in stock?"

Huh. There was always some in the fridge. Even if I didn't buy more. I assumed it was magic. No, it was my brother.

He handed the ice cream to me and fished a spoon out of the bag. Those wonderful people had thought of everything. The last thing I wanted was to go to the kitchen after getting comfortable in my pity position.

I dug in while he waited, watching.

After a few bites, he leaned forward and put his hands on my shoulders.

"Chloe, what's going on?"

There was no point in keeping it in at this point. He could get mad, but it wouldn't change the fact it happened, and it was over.

"I've kept something from you."

His look of concern deepened as his eyes narrowed. "What?"

"Reese."

"Murray?"

I nodded.

"What did he do?" Anger filled his voice. I had to calm him down before he took off in search of blood.

"We were seeing each other."

His face transformed into disbelief, mouth agape and all. "What?"

"We went out a few times. I really liked him."

"How long?"

"Since I took him out that night to show him around."

"That was weeks ago! Why didn't you tell me?"

"Because of this! I knew you would freak out."

"I'm not freaking out because you were dating Murray. I'm mad you didn't tell me."

"What?"

He shook his head. "I can't believe you would think that little of me, Chloe."

His words were a punch to the gut. "I'm sorry."

"Me too. I'm sorry for whatever I did to make you think you couldn't trust me. That you couldn't tell me. That you thought I would be anything but happy for you."

He started to stand, but I grabbed his arm and pulled him back down. "I'm sorry. I was scared."

"Of what?"

"That you would be mad. That you'd take it out on him. That it would mess things up for the team. That the guys would be mad at me. That the guys I'd turned down would call me a hypocrite. That the office would find out and fire me. That people would find out and call me a jersey chaser."

He stayed silent. I'd unloaded quite a bit on him.

"I can't believe you would think so little of everyone around you. Everyone on the team loves you. Everyone in the office loves you. I love you." He stared me down until I started crying again. "Hey."

He wrapped his arms around me and took the ice cream from my trembling hand. "I'm sorry. I'm not mad at you. I'm just a little shocked."

He rubbed my back until I calmed down. "You can tell me anything. I don't want you to keep secrets. I know I hadn't been easy on Reese, but I wanted to push him. I wanted him to prove to us and to himself that he has what it takes to be on the team."

"Really?"

"Yeah. I know I was hard on him, but he's a good guy."

I blinked away the tears and sighed.

"So, what happened?"

"I didn't want to tell anyone about us. When you called and I told you I was going out with the girls, he wasn't happy. He didn't want to keep lying to you."

He smirked, and I punched his arm. "This isn't about you."

"I know. I'm just glad to hear that. It means he respects me." I glared at him. "But it's more about you. He probably knew how hard it was on you."

I nodded. "He did."

"He was trying to do the right thing." He paused. "Wait! That was why he kissed you!"

I giggled and nodded.

"Son of a—"

I swatted at him. "Hey. Be nice. He lied that night, and I got hurt."

"That's why you left early?"

"Yeah."

"Then you turn around and do the same thing to him?"

When he said it like that, it was pretty stupid.

"How do you feel about him right now?"

I looked down at my lap, wishing I could take my ice cream and run to my room. I didn't want to talk about how I felt about him. It hurt.

"You love him?"

"What?" There was no way.

"I don't think you'd be this upset if it were just casual for you. And I don't think he would have been upset about what you said to me if he didn't care as much."

"We've only known each other for a few weeks."

"It can happen in less time."

"I told myself I wouldn't end up with a player."

"We're not that bad."

I nudged him. "No, you guys are pretty great."

"Then why are you sitting here eating garbage and crying to me?"

"What do you mean?"

"You should be going after him."

I shook my head. "I can't."

"Why?"

"He doesn't want to be with me anymore."

"I don't think that's true. I think he wants to be with you so much that he doesn't want to keep it a secret anymore."

"Really?"

He nodded.

"What should I do?"

"Give him the night to cool off. Plus, you're not looking your best."

I stuck out my tongue and he laughed. "You just proved my point."

"Go to bed. Things will look better in the morning."

I stood and narrowed my eyes at him. "Since when are you the wise one?"

He smirked. "Since you lost it. One of us has to be sane."

"Whatever." I reached for my beloved ice cream, but he brushed my hand away.

"I'll clean up out here. Just go to bed."

I eyed him but gave in. I didn't have the energy to argue.

"Thanks, Erik."

He nodded and pointed at the hall. "Go."

I followed his orders even though part of me hated letting him boss me around. It was nice to have the roles reversed. I'd spent most of my adult life taking care of him. I'd let him do it for once.

28

REESE

I drove around the city for hours until finally heading home. I wanted to go back to her house. I wanted to run up the stairs and take her in my arms. I wanted to kiss away the hurt and confusion. This wasn't something we couldn't work through. I could be more patient. I could wait to tell everyone. I was willing to do that. I wasn't willing to lose her.

I'd give her the night. I'd give us both time to recoup and calm down. Time to think.

I lay in bed, staring at the ceiling until four in the morning. Since sleep wasn't an option, I got up, changed, and headed to the arena for a workout.

No one was here yet. Obviously.

I racked a squat rack with weights and got to work.

Two hours, and hundreds of reps later, a water bottle hit me in the side of the head. I pulled out my headphones and looked around.

"Hey, idiot."

Erik.

Great.

I turned to see him standing directly behind me.

"I figured you'd be here."

I narrowed my eyes. "Why?"

"You weren't home, and you don't really know anyone else in the area."

I shrugged, not wanting to admit he was right. If I wasn't at home I was here. Or with Chloe, but I wasn't going to admit that.

"Wait, how did you know I wasn't home?"

"That was the first place I checked."

"Why were you looking for me?"

He didn't seem angry, mostly annoyed.

"I wanted to talk to you."

"About?"

"Chloe." He knew.

"What about her?"

"You're an idiot."

I couldn't argue that.

"You never should have let her go."

"She told you?"

He sat on the bench next to me and began curling a dumbbell. "Yeah. While she was crying and eating ice cream last night."

I hated knowing I'd made her cry, but he didn't seem to mind rubbing it in.

"So, you're here to kill me?" It made sense. Why else would he be searching for me? Holding a thirty-pound object he could easily aim at my head.

He chuckled, did two more reps, and set down the weight. "Why do you guys think I'm going to hurt you?"

I stared at him. Really? He hadn't exactly made my life easy since I got here.

"Alright. I get it. But she's my sister. I want her to be happy, even if that means being with you."

"Really?" I was still ready to spring to my feet and run at any moment.

"Yes, Murray."

"You don't want to duel or something?"

"Seriously?"

I shrugged.

"I know I haven't been the most inviting person, but I wanted to see what you could do. I wanted you to work for it. I wanted to see if you could step up and be a part of the team."

"Did I?"

"I wouldn't be sitting here if you hadn't."

"Why are you sitting here?"

"Because my sister is hurting, and I can't fix it."

Did he think I could? I doubted she wanted to see me.

"I love my sister more than life itself. She's the most important person in the world to me. And for some reason, she cares about you."

"She does?" I knew I sounded like an idiot, but I was shocked I was having this discussion. Never in my wildest imagination would I have ever pictured Erik Schultz and I having a deep conversation.

"Yes. I think you two need to have a long talk."

"I doubt she wants to speak to me."

"She will. She needs to know you're there."

He resumed his workout like we hadn't just had a moment.

By the time I finished, the rest of the team had arrived, so I changed and put my gear on for practice.

I tried to push Chloe out of my mind. I needed to focus on the drills and make sure we were ready for our next game tomorrow. I needed to, but I couldn't. Erik's words were on loop in my mind. She told him about us. He didn't want to kill me. Did that mean if we were together it would be out in the open? Was she ready for that? Or had she just had a bad night and told her brother?

There was only one way to find out.

During a water break, I scanned the seats looking for her. I found the Pride, but didn't see her. Emma shook her head when I met her eyes. Chloe wasn't there. It was the first time she wasn't watching practice. I looked to Erik and saw him doing the same thing.

She was never here for me. She was supporting her brother.

Knowing I was the reason she wasn't here now made me sick. I was selfish to push her. She wasn't ready, and I should have respected that. I hated that now I was keeping her from cheering for Erik. I knew how much it meant to him. Olli had told me that she'd never missed a game or practice since Erik signed. Even if she had class back at the beginning. She was always there for him, until today.

Coach finally blew the whistle and let us go. I showered and changed in record time. Hartman yelled at me on my way out the locker room door, but I ignored him. I was on a mission.

I entered the elevator and closed my eyes until I got to the front office. I blew out a breath and ignored everyone around me. I would not be deterred.

I was almost to her office when Kristen popped up from her cubical. She narrowed her eyes and slowly shook her head. Great. Erik was fine, but now I had to get through a hundred-pound ball of anger.

"Is she in?"

"Nope." She popped the p like she was smacking gum.

I looked at the office. The door was closed but the light was on.

"Liar."

I grabbed the knob and turned it as Kristen leaped to block me. I dodged her and slipped in the room.

"I tried to stop him!" I shut the door before she could get in and maul me.

Chloe was sitting at her desk with a folder covering her face.

"Hey."

She lowered it until just her eyes were showing. Her red, swollen eyes.

My heart fell to my feet. I'd done that.

"What?"

"I didn't see you at practice."

"I was there."

"Emma said you weren't."

"I didn't sit with them."

That didn't make sense. She always sat with her friends.

"Were you hiding?"

Her eyes narrowed. "No. I had work to do and I didn't want them to distract me, so I sat in the upper bowl."

She was avoiding me.

"I'm sorry, Chloe."

The folder lowed an inch.

"For what?"

I let out a breath. "That's a long list."

"I've got time."

I almost laughed. Her sass was still there. "I'm sorry I pressured you to tell. I'm sorry I didn't respect your decision to keep it to ourselves. I'm sorry I didn't come back last night. I'm sorry I didn't talk to you about it. I'm sorry I hurt you. It's the last thing I ever wanted to do."

The folder lowered again.

"Then why didn't you come back?"

I rubbed my face, giving myself time to think. I wanted to. Why didn't I? I was scared. "I didn't want you to tell me it was all over."

She finally set the folder down. "I thought it was."

"What? No."

"It seemed like you were done."

"I just needed time to think."

"You left me, Reese." Her voice broke and I was up out of my seat. I hurried around her desk and pulled her into my arms. I kissed the top of her head and stroked her hair while she fell apart.

It was the most painful thing in the world. I'd take a thousand hits against the boards to take away her tears. Each one destroyed me.

"Chloe, please."

She sobbed, and I scooped her into my arms and sat so she was in my lap. I tightened my arms around her and waited. I didn't know what else to do.

Erik's words ran through my mind. She needed to know I'm here.

"Chloe, I'm never going to leave again. I promise."

She sniffed and looked up at me with watery eyes. "You won't?"

I kissed her wet cheeks and nodded. "I'm not going anywhere."

She sighed and leaned into me. It was the best feeling in the world.

"You can try to get rid of me, but I won't go."

"I don't want you to."

"Good." I kissed her forehead.

I wanted a few moments for her to calm down. "Erik didn't kill me."

She giggled. "I can see that."

"I don't think the other guys will either."

She shook her head. "I don't think they will."

"Do you want to tell them?"

She nodded against my chest. "I want everyone to know."

I kissed her again. I wanted everyone to know she was mine.

29

CHLOE

It was Reese's idea. If things went bad, I was blaming him.

Under no circumstance had I ever thought I'd be standing in front of the entire team plus the coaches. Even the equipment manager was waiting.

"Thanks for giving us a moment of your time. We won't be long. I know we need to warm up."

"Out with it, Murray," Coach Rust yelled from near the door.

Reese looked down at me for a second before facing the group.

"Seriously, Murray. Stop dragging this out." Erik stood. "He's dating my sister." He turned toward us. "Can we go now?"

I nodded as he walked past me muttering something about drama queens.

Hartman stood and hugged me before patting Reese's back. "Treat her right."

He didn't need to elaborate on the warning that filled

those words. The team would be watching out for me, even if it meant turning on one of their own.

"I will."

Hartman nodded and waved to the rest of the guys. "Stop sitting around, you lazy piles of garbage. We have a game to win."

The rest of the players passed us, offering their congratulations to me and threatening Reese with their words or looks.

Not a single one of them was mad. No one said anything to me about breaking my rules or asking why I made an exception for him.

Erik was right. I needed to give them all more credit. At the end of the day, we're family. We want each other to be happy, no matter what that means.

I fought the tears from emerging. I'd told myself since my parents died that it was just me and Erik. That's all I had.

What a lie.

I had twenty-two brothers, not including the coaches and my coworkers in the front office. They were my family.

Not by blood, but by everything that mattered.

Reese turned to me after the room emptied and wrapped his arms around me. "Thanks for doing this, Chloe."

I pressed against him. "I'm sorry I didn't do it sooner."

"It worked out exactly how it was supposed to." He kissed the top of my head before stepping back. "I've got to go warm up."

"I'll see you soon."

I stood up on my toes and kissed him before leaving.

When I got to my seat, Emma was waiting. "How did it go?"

"They were all happy for us."

She laughed. "I told you so."

She did. She'd been right. Reese had been right. I just needed to learn a lesson.

The sea of black and red around me began yelling as the guys skated on to the ice. I watched them as they passed me, grateful for each of them.

They looked good. I could tell they were eager to start. The energy in the building was tangible. The countdown to the start of the game was nearly over and the guys returned to their bench.

Emma looped her arm around my waist and pulled me over. "You're looking pretty happy."

"I am." It was a relief to get everything out in the open, and I couldn't wait for the game to end. I wanted to run into his arms without worrying who saw us. I wanted to go out with the team and be able to sit next to him without raising questions.

"Good." She winked and stepped back to clap as Olli was announced. She was a woman in love, and she didn't hide it.

I wanted to be like her.

The crowd was unbelievable. I could barely hear the women around me. It was exactly what the guys needed to get in the right mindset. They loved when the fans took over the arena. They were used to it, but it could overwhelm the other team.

Hopefully Reese was used to it after the first game.

I couldn't keep my eyes off him through the national anthem. He looked calm, ready.

When the first line took their positions, Erik passed him, and they exchanged a nod and Erik patted him on the back.

If anyone asked, I would have told them I was smiling because I was excited for the game. The truth was embarrassing. I was the happiest I'd been in years. All because my boyfriend and my brother were getting along.

At this rate, I'd be crying the first time Erik invited Reese over to the house.

Hartman faced off for the first puck drop and won it for the Fury. The game was a fast one. The Minnesota Ice were known for playing quick. The guys looked good though. I knew they loved a challenge, and this team wanted to push them.

Neither team scored for the first ten minutes. It was heated, but no one was getting too physical yet. I stood when Erik and Reese traded back onto the ice. They'd been working together seamlessly this game.

"Come on, boys!"

Emma stood with me and cheered.

Malkin, one of our defensemen, stole the puck from an Ice player before he had a chance to shoot and passed it to Erik.

Erik skated into the Ice's zone. Reese was behind him, on the far side, ready. Erik passed the puck to Reese, who swung and sent the puck flying toward the goalie. I held my breath as it soared. The goalie went high, and the puck flew under his glove.

I grabbed Emma and began jumping around while everyone in our area screamed around us.

It was an incredible shot. One that would live in the team's highlights for years.

Reese and Erik were bombarded by the rest of the guys on the ice. They skated over to their bench, bumped fists with their teammates, then Reese broke away. He skated directly to me, took off his helmet and said, "I love you." He pointed to me and smiled.

My jaw must have been on the floor. Emma nudged me. "Smile or say it back. Don't just stand there."

I snapped out of my daze. "I love you, too!" I screamed as loud as I could. The people around us turned to see who he was talking to. I waved to him and they turned their cheers to me.

I knew my face was bright red, and I prayed the cameras weren't on me. They would be on him. They always followed the person who scored.

Wonderful. The first time we say I love you to each other is on national television.

This was what it meant to be with a player.

And it was completely worth it.

30

CHLOE

Two months later

"Show me your hand!" Emma jumped from her seat and reached for me. I offered my right hand, but she swatted it away. "Your left hand!"

I held it up and immediately her smile disappeared. "Seriously?"

"Sorry to disappoint you." I sat next to her and greeted the ladies around me.

"I thought he was going to ask for sure."

She was so upset I couldn't help but laugh. "We've known each other for less than six months, Emma. That would be way too fast."

"Oh stop. You two are meant to be together. It's going to happen eventually, so why put it off?"

I sighed. "Because things are still new. We're enjoying this time."

She shook her head, but Sophia sat next to me and smiled. "Good. Take your time. Marriage is forever."

I nodded. "See, Emma."

She waved her hand and kept her eyes on the guys. This was the first practice after the three-day break for Christmas. We'd been lucky enough to have time to go to Michigan to visit Reese's family. Erik even came with us. He'd been so supportive of us and wanted to get to know Reese's parents. It wasn't a secret that Reese and I were planning on getting married, eventually, and Erik wanted to make sure his family was worthy of me. His words.

It was nice of him. I'd never say it to him, but I was pretty sure he craved having a family for the holiday. The Murrays opened their home and heart to both of us, and now Erik kept in touch with Carl and Karen. He'd become a surrogate son to them, and he reveled in their attention.

"How was your Christmas?" I nudged her elbow. Time to move onto a safer topic.

"It was really good." Her eyes glinted with something.

"What happened?" I studied her face for any hints.

"Oh, nothing. We just got some good news."

So that's how she was going to play it. "Fine. Don't tell me."

She laughed. "We will soon."

Sophia leaned across me. "You better not be moving."

Emma shook her head. "No! I wouldn't be happy about that at all."

"Good." Sophia settled back. "I wish the guys had more time off. I would have loved to visit my family."

"Did you stay here?" I felt bad that I couldn't remember her plans.

"We were supposed to go to Vail, but at the last minute his parents showed up. As a surprise."

She bit out the last part, obviously unhappy about her in-law's appearance.

"Oh sorry." I cringed. I wouldn't have minded, but I'd learned Sophia wasn't big on surprises.

"It's fine. We'll go another time." She shrugged. "It looks like a few of the guys had a bit too much pie over the break."

She pointed out a few who were falling behind in the suicide drill. It was cruel of the coaches to make them do that on their first day back from a break.

"How many do you think will puke?" Emma asked, looking a little too excited at the possibility.

"Four." Sophia sounded confident.

I watched the players closely. Three of them had already failed to get to the other end of the rink before the beep. They had twenty minutes left.

"Six." I felt bad betting against them. I wouldn't want to be in their shoes...well, skates.

"I'll go for five." Emma held out her hand and we all shook on it.

"Go faster, Carlisle!" Emma screamed at the poor guy in dead last.

"Don't be mean." I couldn't help but laugh when he flipped her the bird as he passed.

She shrugged. "It'll toughen him up."

We continued cheering them on until I felt a tap on my shoulder. I turned and one of the wives was leaning down to talk to me.

"There's a girl who just walked in. None of us have seen her before."

Oh perfect. Way to ruin our game.

"Let me know if anyone barfs." I stood and walked toward the blonde sitting in the front row a few sections away.

She didn't look like the typical girl that showed up uninvited. Her hair fell behind her in waves and she was wearing a simple white shirt with jeans. Not a bimbo at all. I almost felt bad I was going to have to kick her out.

"Hi there." I walked to the end of her row and waited for her to turn.

"Hi." She was pretty. Her big blue eyes looked at me skeptically. Almost as if she was judging whether or not *I* should be there.

"Can I help you?"

She was throwing me off. They normally panic by now.

"No, I'm fine."

Huh. "Well, this is a closed practice. We don't allow the public to watch, but you can come back on Wednesday for the open one."

She narrowed her eyes. "Excuse me?"

"Look, I'm sure you're a fan and we appreciate it, but I have to ask you to leave."

She laughed and turned back to the ice. "Go for it."

I looked up to the security guard at the portal. He was watching the players. Why wasn't he coming down? He knew the drill. If they didn't move on their own, security intervened.

"I'm only going to ask one more time before I have security remove you. Please leave."

She smirked. "I don't think so."

The guard still wasn't moving.

"What's your name."

She looked up at me and smiled sweetly. "Madeline Romney."

I pursed my lips and eyed her. Romney, as in Coach Romney? He had an older daughter, but she lived in Chicago.

Why hadn't anyone told me she was coming back?

A whistle blew on the ice grabbing my attention. Coach was skating toward us waving with the whistle still in his mouth. He came up to the glass beaming...like a proud dad.

"Hi, honey!" I heard him over the sound of blades on the ice.

Great.

"Hi, Dad!" Madeline waved, then looked to me. "Do I still need to leave?"

"Of course not." I waved to him and took a seat next to her. "You could have led with that."

She laughed. "And miss your reaction? I thought flames were going to fly from your head."

"I wasn't that bad."

She turned to face me. "No, but I don't think you like being ignored."

"Not really." I shrugged. "So, you're Coach's daughter."

"Yup. Who are you married to?"

My jaw dropped, and she snickered. "I'm not."

"Not yet?"

"What? No. I'm Erik Schultz's sister."

Her eyebrow shot up. "Nice."

"And I'm dating Reese Murray."

Her other brow raised. "So I wasn't that far off."

"No." I shook my head. This girl was going to keep me on my toes. "How long are you here?"

"Who knows."

"You aren't visiting?"

She shook her head. "Nope. We just moved here."

"We?"

"Me and my boyfriend."

I looked over at Coach Romney. How did he feel about that?

"Well, welcome to the family." I pointed over to where I'd been sitting. "That's the Pride. You're more than welcome to join us whenever you're here. We have a section reserved for games too, so let me know if you'll be there and I'll reserve you a seat."

"Thanks. I usually watch with my mom, though."

Duh. Of course, she did.

"Right. Well, the offer stands." I stood. "It was nice to meet you, Madeline."

"You too..."

"Chloe."

I waved and walked back to the Pride.

"Who was that?" They were all asking the same question, so I addressed the group.

"That's Madeline Romney, Coach's daughter. She just moved here, so be sure you make her feel welcome."

A few of the women stood immediately and left to sit with her. We didn't like new people floating around, but the minute we discovered they were family, they were welcomed with open arms.

"So, any pukers?"

Emma nodded. "Three so far."

I scanned the ice and saw Erik, Reese, Porter, and Olli leading the group. At least it wasn't any of our guys. I watched them stay together as they glided to each goal line.

When the final whistle blew, Sophia was the winner. She did a little dance and demanded we each bring her candy at the next practice as her prize.

Reese skated up to the glass and removed his helmet.

I waved, and he smiled.

"I love you!" He yelled so the whole group could hear him. I shook my head and wished my face wasn't turning red. He'd taken every opportunity to tell me in front of people. Not that I minded the public declarations. It was just going to take some getting used to.

"I love you."

He smiled and turned to head to the locker room. Erik was waiting for him, shaking his head.

I couldn't keep the smile off my face. There was nothing better than seeing the two men I cared about most in the world getting along, especially when I thought it would never, ever happen.

Thanks for reading! I hope you enjoyed Reese and Chloe's story!
Word of mouth is so important for authors to succeed. If you enjoyed PUCK DROP, I'd love for you to leave a review on Amazon!

Keep Reading,
Xoxo B

ABOUT THE AUTHOR

Brittney has been an avid reader for as long as she can remember. Her parents' form of punishment growing up was taking away her books and making her go outside to play. She loves the beach, exercising, sleeping in, and cookies. Yes, she does know those contradict each other. She's an obsessive dog lover and is slowly learning to appreciate the mountains she lives in. Nature can be okay, sometimes.

Find out more about Brittney and her books at
www.Brittneymulliner.com

Made in the USA
Columbia, SC
24 April 2020